UNICEF
Book of
CHILDREN'S
Legends

UNICEF
Book of
CHILDREN'S

compiled and wit

STACKPOLE BOOKS

legends

photographs by

William I. Kaufman

Adapted for English-reading children by
ROSAMOND V. P. KAUFMAN

Because the language of a
child's heart is universal, the
photographs and legends have been
arranged to complement
each other according to the meaning
of each and not according to the
country from which each comes.

UNICEF BOOK
OF CHILDREN'S LEGENDS
Copyright © 1970 by William I. Kaufman
Published by
STACKPOLE BOOKS
Cameron and Kelker Streets,
Harrisburg, Pa. 17105, U.S.A.

Library of Congress Catalog Card Number:
74-110475
ISBN 0-8117-1805-0
Printed in U.S.A.

ontents

Introduction

Legends and folk tales form a very important part of the national literature in most countries of the world. Handed down by word of mouth from generation to generation they are a precious heritage which the old give to the young. They express the distinct thoughts, feelings, beliefs, joys, dreams and hopes of each of the nations in which they are born; yet there are certain threads that bind them together. Some of them speak of the heroic deeds of historic characters; others give us a glimpse of the world of the supernatural—talking turtles, dragons, magic birds; still others tell of lives we can never live in the realms of fairy kings, queens and Indian gods. There are legends in which animals seem to live the lives of men and men seem to take on the behavior of the animals.

Legends entertain and stimulate the imagination, but they also teach us something about the meaning of life. There are folk tales about parents and children, about those who govern and those who serve, about success and failure, justice and injustice, hatred and love—all the extremes that have made men think, act and cause change.

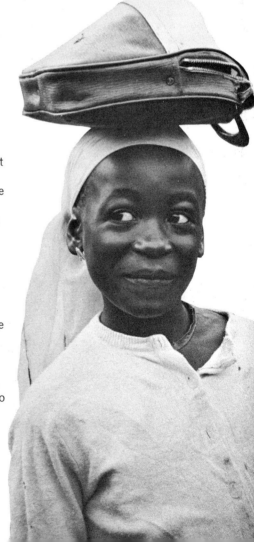

The roots of a people are revealed in legend. For centuries children have listened and learned from legends that instructed them in the ways of their own culture. Now these folk tales have been sought out and written down by devoted scholars, and it is our turn to listen and learn not merely about our own culture but about the cultures in nations far beyond our own. When we do, we see that we have interesting "differences" to share with each other. Legends reveal the uniqueness of the land from which they come. They show us that sometimes our differences bind us more closely to each other than our similarities; for when we read these pages we can experience the same emotions, the same excitement, the same anticipation, the same amusement and the same joy, no matter what land we come from, and no matter what language we speak.

The language of the legend is universal. It is the language of the past, but it is also the language of the future.

WILLIAM I. KAUFMAN

Five White Eag

The Origin of the Sierras Nevadas de Mérida

(Venezuela)

One day five white eagles were flying across the blue sky. Their enormous bodies, resplendent with feathers, threw long shadows on the hills and the mountains. Did they come from the north? Did they come from the south? Indian tradition tells us only that five white eagles came from the starry sky long ago. They came in the days of Caribay, nymph of the sweet-smelling forest, first woman among the Mirripuyes, who lived on the top of the steep Andes.

Caribay was the daughter of the fiery Star King, Zuhe, and the pale Moon Queen, Chia. She could imitate the song of the birds. She could run as swiftly through the grass as crystalline water flowing in a brook and she could play with the flowers and the trees like the wind.

When Caribay saw the giant white eagles flying across the sky with their feathers shining in the sunlight like sheets of silver, she wanted to dress herself in their rare and splendid plumage. Without rest she chased the shadows of the enormous birds. She crossed deep valleys, climbed through woods and traveled through forests,

Photo: Tur

searching and searching. Finally, tired and worn, she rested on a solitary peak of the Andean mountains. On one side she could look down on the broad grassy plains and on the other side she could barely define the outline of the two beautiful gray and emerald forests that ran along the blue arc of the Coquivocoa. The eagles rose ever higher and higher above the mountains until they were lost in space. Their shadows no longer fell upon the earth. Then Caribay crossed from one cliff to the other, through the sloping mountains, watering the ground with her tears. As she wept, the wind carried her voice on high to the ears of her father, the Star King, but he was powerless. The eagles had already disappeared from sight and the sun was sinking in the west.

Stiff with cold, Caribay turned her eyes to the east, calling upon Chia, her mother the pale moon. The winds stilled and around her was a great silence. Stars came out and on the horizon there was a dim semicircular glow. A cry of admiration escaped Caribay's lips and broke the heavy hush of the wastelands. The moon appeared, and by the light of its pearly rays Caribay could see the five white plumed eagles, brilliant and fantastic.

As the birds slowly descended in all their majesty, Caribay, mythical Indian princess of the Andes, sweetly sang her song of the woodlands. She was full of joy as she watched the mysterious birds flutter over the crest of the mountain. Finally they set down, each one clinging to the bare rock of a separate cliff. There they remained—unmoving, silent, their heads turned north, their gigantic wings extended as if they were planning to lift off and disappear once more into the blue sky beyond.

Caribay, anxious to adorn herself with the rare plumage of the eagles, ran towards them to tear off the coveted feathers. But the glacial wind numbed her hands and the eagles became petrified, turning into five immense masses of ice. Caribay gave a scream of terror. Panic-stricken, she fled from the scene.

The moon darkened. The wind howled and whistled through the boulders with a sinister noise. All of a sudden, the five white eagles, bristling in a fury, shook their monstrous wings. The ground was covered with snowflakes and the whole mountain lay cloaked in the white plumage of the five eagles of Mérida.*

---

* According to Indian tradition, the five white eagles are today the five high cliffs of the Andes, always dressed in their mantle of snow. The furious awakening of the eagles causes the violent and tempestuous snowfalls that cover the wasteland; and when the Indians hear the whistling of the wind through the boulders of the mountains, they are reminded of the sad, monotonous woodland cry of Caribay as she calls to her mother, the pale Andean moon.

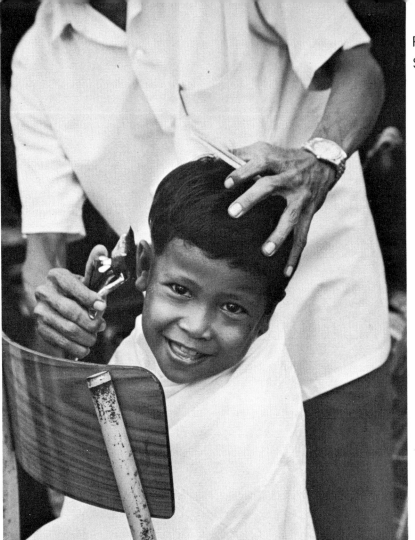

Czar Trojan's Ears

(Yugoslavia)

Once upon a time there lived a czar named Trojan. Trojan had ears like those on a goat. Each day he would call a barber to shave him but none ever returned from the palace for after the barber had done his work the czar would ask, "What do you see, my good man?" and the barber would answer, "I see that the czar has the ears of a goat." When he heard the barber's answer, the czar would order the barber's head to be chopped off at once.

One day the turn fell to a barber who was so frightened for his safety that he pretended to be ill. In his place he sent his young apprentice.

When the apprentice appeared before the czar the unhappy monarch demanded to know why the master artisan had not come himself. The apprentice answered sweetly that his master was ill, whereupon the czar was satisfied and sat down to be shaved.

During his work, the apprentice noticed that Trojan's ears were like the ears of a goat but when the czar asked him what he had observed, the apprentice answered, "I see nothing, Sire."

Trojan gave the apprentice twelve gold ducats and ordered him to come regularly to shave him.

When the apprentice returned home, the artisan was curious and asked him about Czar Trojan. The apprentice reported that the czar was courteous and kind and that he had been ordered to come personally each day to shave the ruler. He showed his master the twelve gold ducats but he said nothing about Czar Trojan's goat's ears.

From that time on the apprentice went each day to shave the czar and each day he received twelve gold ducats. He revealed the czar's secret to nobody, but after many months the apprentice began to worry and grieve. The burden of carrying the czar's secret was growing heavier and heavier on his heart. He grew thinner and thinner. He started to pine and became sad and listless.

The artisan, noticing the change in his ordinarily good-natured pupil, started little by little to put questions to the boy. Finally the young man confessed that he carried in his heart a great secret which he was forbidden to tell anyone in the world.

"If only I could tell my secret to someone, I would be much relieved," said the troubled apprentice.

The artisan was kind, and wanting to help, he said, "Tell me and I shall tell no one; if you are afraid to tell me, go to the priest and tell him; if you can't tell him either, then go out into the fields behind the town. Dig a hole. Put your head into it, and say three times to the earth what you know. Then close the hole and come away."

The apprentice chose to tell his secret to the earth. He went out of the town, dug the hole, put his head into it and said three times, "Czar Trojan has the ears of a goat."

Covering the hole once more with earth, he returned home, tranquil in his heart and mind.

In time, an elder tree grew on the spot where the apprentice had told his secret and from the tree grew three branches as fine and straight as candles.

Photo: Cam

One day some shepherds found the elder tree. One of them cut off a branch and made a fine flute but when the flute began to whistle, instead of a tune, the shepherds heard the flute pipe out "Czar Trojan has the ears of a goat."

With much excitement, the shepherds returned to the town to tell the news. "Czar Trojan has the ears of a goat! Czar Trojan has the ears of a goat!" they whispered to all who would listen.

The news spread like wildfire and soon Czar Trojan himself heard little children in the streets imitating the voice of the flute as it whistled "Czar Trojan has the ears of a goat!"

At once Trojan summoned the apprentice to him and demanded in a fury, "Why did you tell my secret to my people?"

As he was innocent, the poor frightened apprentice was at a loss for words. He implored the monarch to believe that he had told no one and when he saw that the czar would not listen and had drawn his sword in preparation for cutting off his head he cried out in desperation. He confessed that he had told his secret to the earth. He told Czar Trojan how the elder tree had shot up on the spot where he had confided the secret and he recounted the tale of how each flute made from a branch of the tree whistled the secret to the wind.

The czar, being a benevolent man at heart and being exceedingly fond of his young barber, decided to test the truth of the apprentice's words. Calling for his carriage and taking the apprentice with him, Trojan departed in search of the elder tree.

Coming to the spot where the apprentice had told his secret to the earth, they discovered the tree with only one branch left. Czar Trojan ordered the young man to make a flute of the branch and when it was made, he commanded the young man to play upon it. As the czar waited in disbelief, the flute whistled "Czar Trojan has the ears of a goat! Czar Trojan has the ears of a goat!"

Finally Trojan was convinced that on earth nothing can be hidden. He granted life to his barber's apprentice and from that time on gave permission that all men could come to shave him without fear.

Don't be in as great a hurry as your Father

(Algeria)

A valiant slipper maker from Fez waited, with great impatience, for the happy birth of a baby who he hoped with all his heart would be a boy.

He thought to get a bed for the child. For a long time he had been carefully collecting under his bed some good strong boards which he had set aside to use in case the necessity presented itself. He went to the home of his good friend the carpenter.

"Greetings, Father Brik," he said, "Always live in peace. I am bringing you some wood of very fine quality from which I hope you can fashion a cradle. My wife will soon favor us with a child."

"So early! Excellent news! I hope it will be a boy who will enlarge the Moslem community. So be it. Please God, he will be a famous scholar of the Blessed Book."

The master carpenter accepted the boards and promised to carve the most beautiful cradle that had ever been created. After exchanging a thousand polite phrases, the two men parted. Some days later, when his wife began to feel the first sensations of childbirth, the slipper maker ran to the carpenter and he urged him to hurry the work.

"My goodness!" said Master Brik. "Of course, I am already working on it in my head. Be calm, your child will sleep peacefully in his cradle with the blessing of God on high."

About a week later, the good wife gave birth to a lovely boy. The joyful father rushed to the craftsman. Carpenter Brik extended his

Photo: GI

best wishes to the happy papa and said to him, "No doubt, you came to see if your cradle is ready. I am going to give the design some finishing touches. You will have it in a few days. It will really be beautiful. Besides, you see, the wood is a delight to my hands. That is only to tell you that the work is almost ready to be started."

The slipper maker begged him to attack the job quickly since the baby was resting on the ground. The men exchanged smiles and congratulations and they parted.

Every day the slipper maker waited for the cradle which the carpenter had not even begun. Day and night he spoke to him about it. During all this time the infant was growing. First he crawled, then he stood up, took his first steps, ran about and finally started to play with other infants in the neighborhood. Finally he went to school. He had heard that once upon a time his father had ordered a lovely cradle for him and had even gone so far as to take fine wood to the master carpenter. From time to time as he grew to manhood he thought about the cradle but little by little he had no need for this bed. He was a big boy, then a handsome young man, and when his studies were completed his father decided to choose a wife for him.

The young man married, and some time afterward when his young wife was expecting a child, he suddenly remembered the cradle, already ordered from Maallem Brik by his father. The carpenter still had not found time to execute the order.

Soon the new baby would be brightening the household and the young father wanted his child to have a proper bed. He went to Master Carpenter Brik and said, "Greetings! Father Brik, God help you. Some years ago my father gave you some fine boards with which he asked you to make my cradle. Would you be kind enough to hurry the work on it. I will soon be needing it for my own baby whose birth is very close at hand."

"I am happy, my child, to hear such good news," said the old craftsman. As a matter of fact, here are the boards your father left in my care. They are in perfect condition. You can expect to have a magnificent cradle for your child, and in only a matter of a few days, maybe even before the birth of the child, you will be able to carry it home. Please God, it will be used to rock your son."

In vain the young man reminded the carpenter of his promise. The child that was so lovingly expected was born. The young father went to the carpenter's home time and again to beg him to fulfill his obligation. Finally, tired of the young bridegroom's constant insistence, Master Brik turned from his work and said, "Patience, my son. You shall have your cradle soon. But please, I beg of you, don't be in as great a hurry as your father."

Hatemtai

(Pakistan)

"Oh you God-loving people, do give a little something to a lame old man."

Hearing these words, young Salim came outdoors and gave an anna to the old beggar who stood before his house.

Photo: Ethiopia

"My son Hatem, may you always be happy," said the beggar and then he moved on.

Salim was puzzled. He went to his father and said, "Father, Father, when I gave an anna to the lame fakir he called me Hatem. My name is Salim. Why then did he call me Hatem?"

His father smiled and answered, "He had good reason to address you thus, my son. First of all, let me tell you how happy I am for your 'hatemtai.' Ah! I know now, you are going to ask me what 'hatemtai' is. Well! . . .

"Many, many years ago there lived a rich chief who had a young, handsome son by the name of Hatem.

"Hatem was not only handsome in looks but even in his deeds he was worthy. He helped the poor and the weak. He eased their pain and suffering. He gave comfort, food, clothes and money to the needy and was prepared to give his life too, should this be necessary.

"Hatem became known for his goodness and charity and his fame spread far and wide. Finally, when the king of the land heard of him, he was so jealous of the young Hatem that he ordered his soldiers to burn down Hatem's house. He commanded that Hatem be taken prisoner and he proclaimed that Hatem be brought to his court.

"Some of Hatem's friends heard of the king's evil plans and they hurried to warn him. They advised him to leave his home; so Hatem, disguised as a beggar, went for the woods.

"Consequently, when the king's men reached Hatem's abode, they could not find him. They set fire to his property and reported to the king that Hatem was missing.

"The king ordered a royal proclamation to be read in the streets. 'Whosoever brings Hatem to the court, dead or alive, will receive a handsome reward of one thousand gold sovereigns.'

"Now it happened that Hatem, exhausted from his flight, saw a small cave hidden along the edge of the forest. He took shelter there and lay down to rest with his eyes facing the mouth of the cave lest the soldiers should approach. A short distance away he observed a tired, very old woodcutter as he went about putting his axe and bundle of sticks against a tree to rest. Hatem could hear him sigh deeply and say aloud, 'Oh God, were I to meet Hatem now, all my troubles would come to an end!'

"Having overheard his words and observing the woodcutter's sad state, Hatem felt pangs of pity. He came from the cave and spoke.

"'Here stands Hatem before you. Take me to the king and reap your reward.'

"The old man was taken aback and answered, 'Oh, no! my good young man, what makes you think I'd do that? Now go back to the cave for fear that the king's men shall spot you here.'

"Just then, they heard hurried footsteps behind them. Four of the king's men came forward quickly and captured Hatem. Quarreling among themselves, each one vowed that he was the first to have seen Hatem and that he was the one who should receive the reward. They bound Hatem and dragged him before the jealous ruler.

"Then Hatem struggled forward. 'Your Majesty,' he said, 'not these wicked men but an old woodcutter who has remained in the forest is my true captor. It is he who deserves the reward.'

"The king, seeing this brave and stalwart young man for the first time, and hearing him speak so honestly and so fearlessly, was much ashamed of himself. He came down from his throne and embraced Hatem. He asked the young man's forgiveness. Then he appointed him Minister to the King and gave a thousand gold coins to the poor old woodcutter. He dismissed the four greedy soldiers from his army and sent them from the realm.

"And so, to this day, the name of Hatem stands for goodness and honor and 'hatemtai' is another word for charity, my boy."

With these words, Salim's father turned proudly from his son and went about the serious work of the day.

Photo: Turkey

th

KRISHNA

LEGEND

(India)

Krishna was the loveliest child in the world. He was dark and handsome and wore pretty clothes. His hair was tied in a knot on the top of his head and there was always a peacock feather in it. His childhood was full of fun and frolic. He went about the village freely and played with his many friends whom he led into exciting adventures. He liked to play pranks on people or make fun of them, and although his parents were annoyed by his tricks, little Krishna was the darling of all the people.

When he grew to manhood, Krishna became a cowherd. He enjoyed tending the cows and calves and took pleasure in guiding them into the jungle, where there was plenty of grass and water. The jungle was an ideal place where Krishna and his friends, the other cowherds, could play and make merry until it was time to bring the cattle home.

Krishna played the flute very well and all were enchanted by his music. In the jungle he would sit on the branch of a tree and play for the other cowherds who gathered round to listen. Even the cows and calves would stop grazing to draw near and the wild animals became tame at the sweet sounds that came from Krishna's pipe. Whenever he played, men,

Photo: Morocco

women and children stopped their work and ran to him, so beloved was he.

Once a poisonous snake named Kaliyan went into the river Yamuna, drinking place of the cows and cowherds. Soon the river waters were poisoned by Kaliyan's venom and whosoever drank the water from the Yamuna fell dead. All the fish floated lifeless in the water. Crocodiles fled and climbed upon the river banks. There they attacked the animals and damaged the crops. Even the trees along the river withered and dried up. Kaliyan was the deadliest enemy of the territory. All the people complained about him. Everybody feared him.

Little Krishna heard news of the terror that Kaliyan had brought to the land and decided he would punish the evil snake for his wickedness. Alone, he went in search of the culprit. He found him living in the deepest part of the river. Without hesitating a moment, Krishna jumped into the water and swam to Kaliyan's home in the depths.

Kaliyan was annoyed at the little dark boy who tried to disturb him. He rushed at Krishna to kill him with one stroke. Krishna quickly thrust himself up to the surface of the water and Kaliyan followed. In a flash, Krishna got hold of Kaliyan's huge head and stood up on it. The big snake had no chance to bite him. Angry and thwarted, Kaliyan tried to shake Krishna off. He plunged to the bottom of the river; he twisted and turned himself around Krishna and tried to squeeze him to death, but Krishna was able to live without breathing for as long as he wished and after a time Kaliyan was forced to come to the surface for a breath of air. When he did, Krishna started kicking and stamping on the serpent's head. Kaliyan struggled hard against Krishna but he was helpless.

Worried that something terrible might happen to their favorite, hundreds of frightened people gathered on the banks of the Yamuna. How surprised they were to find Krishna dancing happily on top of the snake! Little by little, Kaliyan lost strength. Unable to bear the pain of Krishna's attack, he spit his venom with all his force in a last valiant effort. Krishna continued to kick him until he had released every drop of his poison. Finally Kaliyan gave up. Knowing his end was near, knowing his only hope lay in seeking Krishna's mercy, the wicked snake prayed to Krishna. He begged him to spare his life. He promised to do whatever Krishna should desire.

Krishna heard the prayer. He released Kaliyan from his grip and ordered him to go far away and never return to the Yamuna.

Kaliyan bowed his head before Krishna. Silently he slid from the Yamuna, never to be seen again by the grateful people who cheered Krishna as he swam ashore victorious.

Photo: ⊦

The Magic Teakettle

(Japan)

here was once a priest who was very fond of tea. He always made it himself and was very fastidious about the utensils he used.

One day, wandering through an old junk shop, he found a beautiful iron kettle used for boiling water and making tea. It was rusty but the old priest could detect the beauty of its lines. He bought it and took it back to the temple. There he polished it and when it was nice and shiny he called his three young pupils to him.

"See what a fine iron kettle I bought today," he said. "Now we shall boil water and have some delicious tea." He put the kettle over a charcoal brazier. It got hotter and hotter and suddenly to everyone's surprise, the kettle grew the head of a badger, a long bushy tail and four little feet.

"Ouch!" said the kettle, "it's hot. I'm burning," and it jumped off the fire and began scampering about the room.

The priest was flabbergasted but he didn't want to lose his new kettle.

"Quick," he said to his pupils. "Don't let it get away."

One pupil grabbed a broom, the other a pair of fire tongs and the third a water dipper. The three of them went chasing after the kettle and when they caught it, the head, the tail and the feet of the little badger had disappeared. Instead there was once again just an ordinary iron teakettle.

"This is indeed peculiar," said the priest. "The kettle must be bewitched. We don't want anything like that around the temple. We shall have to get rid of it."

Just at that moment a junkman came into sight. The priest took the kettle out to him and said, "Here is an old utensil I am not using anymore. I shall sell it to you very cheaply. Give me whatever you think it's worth."

The junkman weighed the kettle on his hand scales and then he bought it for a very small sum. He went home whistling because he was very pleased to have struck such a bargain.

That night when the junkman went to sleep the entire house was very still. As he lay in his bed he heard a little voice saying, "Mr. Junkman . . ."

"Who's calling me?" said the junkman, lighting a candle.

There before him he saw the kettle with the little badger head, the bushy tail and the four little feet. He was very taken aback.

"Who are you?" he said. "Are you the kettle I bought at the temple today?"

"Yes, that's me," said the kettle, "but I am not an ordinary kettle. My name is Bumbuku. That means 'good luck.' I am really a badger in disguise. That mean old priest burned me so I ran away. But if you will treat me kindly and take care of me and never put me on a fire, I shall stay with you and help you make a fortune."

"How can you do that?" asked the junkman.

"I know all sorts of wonderful tricks," said the kettle. "You could put me in a show and sell tickets to people who want to see my tricks."

The junkman thought this idea was enticing. The next day he built a little theater and put up a big sign that said: Come See Bumbuku, the Magic Teakettle of Good Luck, and His Extraordinary Tricks.

Each day more people heard about Bumbuku and each day more people came to see him. The junkman sold tickets out front and as soon as the theater was full he would go inside and give Bumbuku the signal on his drum. Bumbuku would come out and do all sorts of acrobatic dances. But the trick that thrilled the crowd the most was when Bumbuku walked across a tight rope carrying a paper parasol in one hand and a fan in the other. The audience cheered and cheered for Bumbuku and after the show the junkman would feed him delicious rice cakes as a reward for his faithful services. The show was so successful that soon the junkman became very, very rich.

One day he said to Bumbuku, "You must be very tired from doing all these tricks. Now we have all the money we need; so why don't I take you back to the temple where you can live peacefully?"

"Well," said Bumbuku, "I am a little tired and I would like to live quietly in the temple but I never want to be put on the fire again and the old priest may never give me delicious rice cakes."

"Have confidence in me," said the junkman.

The next morning, he took Bumbuku, a small sack filled with money, some of Bumbuku's favorite rice cakes, and went to the temple. When they got there the junkman told the priest all that had happened to him and he gave him the little sack filled with money for the temple.

"Would you please let Bumbuku live here quietly, feeding him rice cakes such as these I have brought and never putting him on the fire again?" the junkman enquired. "If you do, I shall leave him here with you."

"Indeed I shall," said the priest, "and he shall have a place of honor in the temple's treasure house. If I had only known that Bumbuku was the magic kettle of good luck, I would never have put him on the fire."

The priest called his pupils and they built a lovely stand on which to put the kettle. On another stand close by they put the rice cakes. Carefully forming a procession, the three pupils, the junkman and the priest carried Bumbuku to the place of honor in the treasure house of the temple and placed the rice cakes at his side.

Some say that Bumbuku is still there in the treasure house of the temple. They say that every day he eats delicious rice cakes and that he is never, never put over a fire. How peaceful he must be. And how happy!

THE **CLAM,** TH

One warm balmy day a large beautiful clam lay on a shallow beach with her shells open and her tongue rolling around aimlessly in her mouth. She was daydreaming and luxuriating in the noonday sun. Just then a young stork flew by. He swooped down and stuck his sharp beak into her tender heart. The clam was shocked. Immediately she slammed her shells shut, catching her enemy's beak between her teeth. The stork flapped his wings. He scratched. He screamed aloud. The harder he pulled, the tighter the clam closed her shell. Finally the stork shrieked for mercy. But in vain. He was caught fast. The clam had no intention of freeing him.

To loosen himself from her grasp the stork resorted to flattery.

"Ah, fair one, do not be so cruel," he said. "I meant only to graze you lightly on your lovely cheek. But alas! in my ardor, my beak slipped and fell into your heart. I did not mean to hurt you. I wanted only to hold you in the protection of my wings. When I feel you clasp me so tightly I cannot describe my passion. Your love consumes me. I feel I am choking. Oh, fair one, release me so that I can breathe a moment."

The clam replied gently, "Oh, how unexpected your attentions are, dear stork. Last night as I slept on the floor of the Dragon King's Glass Palace I dreamed that a beautiful angel with lovely white wings embraced me. He swore that he loved me better than all others in the world and that he would take me to his air castle beyond the Azure Dome. Now I see it was to be you, my darling stork. But

Photo: Uga

before you take me away with you, let us wait until the tide comes in and we shall go to bid my parents farewell." And so saying, the clam clamped the stork more tightly than ever between her teeth.

While they were thus locked in tender embrace, a fisherman came by. He scooped them both up in one hand and threw them into his basket. "What a stroke of good fortune!" he said and strolled along the beach looking for others who were so careless they forgot to watch what was going on about them.

STORK and the FISHERMAN

(Korea)

China Poblana

Many, many years ago in Delhi, India, a little daughter was born to kings. Her mother's name was Borta, which means Fragrant Fruit. The Grand Mogul was her ancestor and her father was a Hindu prince.

When she was still very small she crawled away from the courtyard and was lost near the Jamuna River bordering the palace. Her mother found her among the reeds. The crying of the child was so anguished that she called her Mirra, which means Bitterness.

Some years later, during the Turkish invasion, Mirra's parents fled to a seaport. One day while the child was playing on the beach she was caught and captured by some Chinese pirates who had disembarked there. In her hand the frightened little girl clutched tightly her only possession, a knotted handkerchief holding some sequins and beads that she had collected and which she intended to use to embroider a sari.

While they were on the high seas the pirates frequently fought among themselves, and in one of the quarrels Mirra's arm was wounded. She sobbed in pain and her crying moved the pirates to notice her. They decided to draw lots for her as part of their loot.

When the ship reached the Philippines the pirate who had won her dragged the girl to the marketplace in Manila and sold her as a slave to a Portuguese merchant. At that time Mexico was known as New Spain and the merchant who had acquired Mirra had an order for just such a slave from Doña Margarita Chavez, the wife of

Photo: India

Don Miguel Sosa, who lived in the city of Puebla de los Angeles.

The Portuguese merchant sailed with Mirra on the *Ship of China* to Acapulco, where he handed her over to her new owners.

The beauty and sweetness of the child won the heart of Doña Margarita, who personally took charge of her and saw that she was baptized with the name of Catarina of San Juan in the Church of San Angel Analco. Doña Margarita became her godmother and she gave Mirra as a present a small sewing box into which the little treasure of sequins and beads was deposited. She learned to speak Spanish well and received a fine education. Seeing her so lovely, and fearing that she would be alone in the world when they were gone, Doña Margarita and Don Miguel advised her to marry a young Chinese slave whose name was Domingo. They promised that when they died she would be granted her freedom.

Mirra had adopted the usual dress of the Mexican servants. But remembering the luxuries of her childhood, she decided to cover her simple red woolen wedding skirt with the sequins and the white cotton blouse with flowers embroidered in beads.

When she sewed her treasure so lovingly on her wedding garments Mirra unwittingly created the Mexican national costume, which Domingo completed by giving her a shawl and a pair of satin shoes. In return, Mirra gave Domingo the precious handkerchief that she had brought from India.

The young woman was so kind and good, the townsfolk began to call her China, for her husband's origin, and Poblana, because they considered her to be one of their own.

China Poblana lived to be eighty-two and at her death on the fifth of January, 1688, the people said that the Wise Men from the East had taken Mirra, the Soul of China Poblana, to heaven. She was buried in the Iglesia de La Compañia, where today the inscription can still be read on the wall:

Here lies Catarina de San Juan
Whom the Mogul gave to the earth
And Angelopolis to heaven.

Christmas Flowers

(El Salvador)

Christmas flowers have not always been red. In times long ago the flowers were white. When the rainy season was ended the summer would transform the emerald of the new leaves into the whiteness of foam, of cloud, of fleece, of snow and of innocence.

Around all the ranches the infinite whiteness of the Christmas flowers could be seen, and the Indians offered the blossoms to their gods as symbols of supreme peace.

But war came, and with it came fire, pillaging, killing and carnage. Dense columns of smoke rose over the mountainpeaks in flight from the "brotherhood of men."

Near the dwellings, along all the roads, over all the trails that zigzagged through the hills, the blood ran like the overflowing of rivers and streams. Mercifully the land absorbed that generous blood, and the roots of the flowers drank in the torrent of life's elixir that had been shed so needlessly.

When the first summer came, much to the amazement of the few survivors, near the last remains of the half-deserted ranches, at the edge of all the paths, the Christmas flowers bloomed red, bloodied. It was as though the blood itself was blooming. The Christmas flowers, more human than the human species, offered that blood in purple chalices to the guardian gods.

Since then the Christmas flowers are no longer a supreme white symbol of peace, but instead they have become a brilliant vermilion reminder of the futility of man's sacrifice to the evil causes of war.

Photo: Se

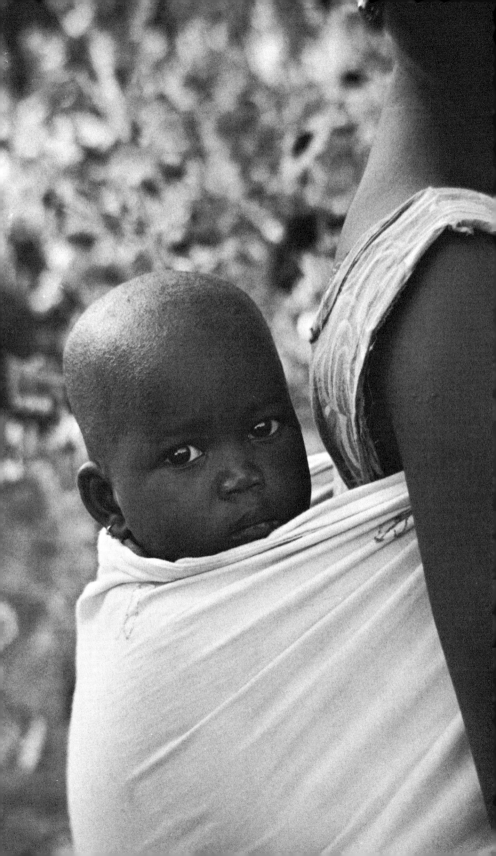

Mr. Tortoise was the cleverest and most cunning animal. Because of this he was given a praise title on the talking drum that went like this:

> **Son of Alika,**
> **The fearsome one,**
> **He who dug in the earth**
> **And struck a water fountain.**

Mr. Tortoise took many other praise titles as well. He was boastful before the world but in private he worried much about losing his wisdom. He feared that his neighbors were jealous and might try to steal part or all of his cunning. He decided to put all his bits of knowledge, tricks and ideas into a gourd with a long slender neck and a round big belly. He then corked it tightly shut. He tied a tough piassava string to the neck of the gourd and passed it round his own neck so the gourd hung down on his chest. Mr. Tortoise found the tallest tree in the middle of the forest. In the dead of night he proceeded to climb to the top, but since the gourd hung down in front of him, he could not get a good grip on the trunk of the tree and he fell down with each attempt he made. All night long he toiled without success.

Mr. Duiker* came past early in the morning.

"Good morning, Mr. Tortoise," said he. "What are you sweating at so early this morning?"

"Hello, Mr. Duiker," answered the Tortoise. "Thank you for asking. I have all that is precious to me tucked inside this gourd. I plan to hang it up on top of this tree. My problem is how to get it there."

"That is easy," said Mr. Duiker. "All you need to do is place the gourd behind instead of in front of you and climb. Then you can get a firm grip on the trunk of the tree with no trouble. Once you get to the top, you can turn the gourd round and fasten it to a branch."

Mr. Tortoise did as he was advised and soon reached the top of the tree. Once there, however, he realized that he was not as clever as he had thought. Even the humble Mr. Duiker was able to solve a problem that he, Mr. Tortoise, could not tackle! He felt so disgusted with himself that he let the gourd drop to the ground, where it broke into a thousand pieces.

And that is how wisdom was scattered all over the universe and why every man, woman, boy and girl is able to pick a little bit of it up for himself, but it is also why no one man has ever been able to learn all that there is to know.

---

* Duiker: a small African antelope

The Chicken

(Thailand)

A long time ago a poor farmer and his wife lived far from town in a small house. One evening the god Indra, dressed as a monk, came to their house and asked, "May I stay here tonight?"

"Yes," they said, "please stay with us."

But the man and his wife were very poor, and they were sad because they had no food for the monk. They did not know what to do. Suddenly the wife thought of something. She said to her husband, "We have a young hen and six chickens. We can cook the hen and give it to the monk in the morning."

The hen heard this. She woke up her young chickens and said, "Tomorrow I shall die. You must be good chickens. Do not be afraid." The young chickens were so sad that they cried for a long time.

Early the next morning the wife said to her husband, "Get the hen."

He killed the hen and pulled out its big feathers. Then he held it over the fire to burn the small ones. The young chickens wanted to die with their mother; so they jumped into the fire. When this happened, the man and his wife were very sad. They gave all of the food to the monk. They did not want to eat any of it. The monk saw their sad faces and asked, "What is wrong?"

"We killed our hen," they told him. "Then her chickens jumped into the fire and died too."

The monk understood. He blessed the farmer and his wife and the hen and chickens.

The god Indra made the hen and her chickens into seven stars in the sky, and today they are called the Chicken Stars or Pleiades.

Stars

Photo: Yugoslavia

The Valley

*I*n days of old a great and wise priest of the Itzaes tribe came before the king. Presenting himself with humility, he bowed low before his ruler and spoke. "Your Excellency, your son the prince, future king of our tribe, must begin to prepare himself if he is to be a kind, wise and courageous leader. The Gods of the Sky have spoken to me. They have given me their prophecy and they have asked me to announce to you that days of war and pain will soon come to our people."

"Who would dare to defy my power?" asked the proud king. "None of the small tribes who are vassals of this great nation would dare to fight my warriors."

Thoughtfully, the all-knowing priest replied, "The days will come, oh my king, days when your eyes will rest in the shade, when un-

known warriors will come from beyond the forests. They will come from beyond the river of life where the ancient grandmother kneaded the corn that gave birth to our nation. They will be blond men, blond as the rays of the sun, and with spears and with fire they will destroy our family."

The king was much grieved when he heard the words of the wise priest and he said, "Oh my respected counselor, you paint a dark future. What can my son the prince do to prevent such a catastrophe?"

"I do not know for certain, great king," replied the sage, "but it would be wise to send him to the heart of the forest, where he can meditate and where he will be able to receive inspiration from our gods."

Heeding the advice of the wise man and with a heavy heart, the king sent the young prince of the Itzaes into the heart of the forest, beyond the lake which surrounded the island. He sent him alone with only a bow and arrow for protection.

The first day the prince traveled through the forest alert to every sign of danger. He ate the fruit of the trees and slept near the fire to ward off the beasts that prowl in the night.

On the second day a torrential rain drove him to seek shelter in a dark cave. At first he feared the cave might be the den of a fox, but when he entered he found it empty. All day it rained and the young prince remained warm and dry in the cave while he meditated and prayed. He begged the Spirit of All Wisdom to help him find an honorable way to save his people from the cruel prophecies of the gods. As night drew on he made a fire with flint and lit a torch of resinous wood. Much to his surprise, when the cave was illuminated, he saw that a beautiful array of colors was reflected from the walls. The entire cavern seemed to be a palace of light.

Attracted by the changing light and shade of these dazzling colors, the prince roved around the cave. Suddenly he discovered an entrance to another cave, bigger and more beautiful than the first. When he examined the strange form of the second cavern more closely, he found it to be a tunnel. Brave and daring, the prince

to: Tunisia

flung himself into the adventure of exploring the tunnel to its very end. Though he was courageous, he was also prudent and along the way he was careful to make marks that would enable him to find his way back to the entrance.

On the dawn of the third day, after much walking, the prince came to the end of the tunnel. Standing at the mouth of the cave, he found himself bathed in a stream of sunlight. Before him lay the splendorous view of a vast hidden valley protected all around by high rock walls and nourished by a clear, swift-running river.

Ecstatic, he admired all that lay before his eyes and, raising his hands and voice to the heavens, he thanked the Father of All Beings for permitting him to discover a corner of Paradise. Filled with delight, he knew that it was time for him to return home.

Imagine the prince's sadness when he was told that his father, the king, had fallen ill and lay dying. He hurried to his father's bedside.

"Dear father," he said, "I bring you news."

Weak with sickness, the king looked into the eyes of his son.

"My child, what news do you bring me? Have the gods inspired you? Have they shown you the course that you must take to save our people?"

"Oh, my father," answered the prince, "the gods have guided me well. I have seen the beautiful caves in the bowels of the earth. The gods have led me to a hidden valley. Only I can find the entrance. If the courage and valor of our warriors should not be enough to save us from the invaders, we shall hide in the valley. There our old men shall rest in the shade, our cornfields will grow and our trees will bear fruit to keep radiant the joy of our maidens."

The wise old priest who had come to give comfort to the king in his last moments was astonished at all the prince had said. Trembling with emotion, he approached the prince and said, "The gods have revealed to you, my prince, the secret road along which the venerated Mayan priests walked when they went to their devotions in the Temple of Chichen Itza. They have shown you the Valley of Rest. From the Valley is a road that is said to continue underground. It leads under the lake and out into the open field that lies before the Temple of the Sun."

Hearing these words, the once strong fearless king looked first at his counselor, then at his son. Smiling peacefully, he said, "Now I shall go to take my rest in the shade. I see, my son, that the gods will preserve the seed of my race. Let me join you in marriage to the lovely Princess Flower of May so that you can live happily and reign over our island until the day when our people must take refuge in the Valley of Rest beyond the caverns of Jobitzinaj."

AUNTY

(Afghanistan)

Once upon a time there was a betel nut, called Aunty. One fine day she washed herself, put on her cleanest dress and went outdoors for a walk. Along the way she met a man riding a horse. He greeted her and said, "Where are you going, Aunty Betel Nut?"

Smiling sweetly, Aunty Betel Nut replied, "I am going to find a husband."

"Would you marry me?" said the rider.

Betel Nut asked, "When you become angry with me, what will you use to beat me?"

"I shall use my riding crop," answered the man.

Aunty Betel Nut turned her face away and said, "I shall not marry you," and she continued her strolling until she came upon a farmer. The farmer asked, "Where are you going, Aunty Betel Nut?"

"I am going to find myself a husband," she replied.

BETEL NUT

Photo: India

The farmer asked, "Would you marry me?"

Betel Nut said, "Tell me, when you become angry with me, what will you use to beat me?"

"I shall beat you with my shovel," said the farmer.

"Then I shall not marry you," said Aunty Betel Nut and went on her way.

Along came a lion. The lion asked Aunty Betel Nut where she was going and her reply was the same as always. When she asked the lion what he would use to beat her with were she to marry him, he replied, "I shall tear you to pieces with my paws."

Carefully Aunty Betel Nut refused his kind offer of marriage and hurried on her search for the perfect mate.

The next ones to come promenading by were a fox, an elephant and a camel. Each one asked for Betel Nut's hand in marriage and each time she asked about their anger and their plans for beating her when they became angry. She was given a choice of being bitten by the strong teeth of the fox, being trounced by the powerful trunk of the elephant or being trampled underfoot by the haughty camel, all of which she politely refused.

Toward nightfall, she met a mouse scurrying across the field.

"Where are you going, Aunty Betel Nut?" squeaked the mouse.

"I am going to find myself a husband," she answered.

"Would you marry me?" asked the mouse.

Betel Nut blinked and asked, "When you are angry with me, what will you use to beat me?"

Quickly the mouse answered, "I shall beat you with my soft little tail."

For a moment Aunty Betel Nut stood very still and then shyly she said, "Then I shall surely marry you."

And so the mouse and Aunty Betel Nut were married and lived happily ever after.

Photo: Lebanon

The Love of the Skunk

(Bolivia)

Once upon a time there was a skunk called Anathuya. He was a likable little animal with a longish face, brown and white striped fur and a lovely bushy tail from which it was unbelievable that he gave off such an intolerable odor.

A story told by the Indians recounts how one day Anathuya was feeling very downhearted. His eyes which were usually bright and sparkling had turned sad and he could hardly touch a morsel of food.

The other animals noticed the change in him and since they had more Christian charity than most men, they tried to distract him and find out why he was so forlorn.

They asked him and asked him but he could only answer by turning his eyes to the heavens.

One evening when Anathuya was sadder than ever, several little animals came to him and urged him, with much fussing and licking of his face, to tell them why he was suffering so deeply.

"Oh, my brothers," he answered, "for several days I have realized that I am in love and if you see that I am sadder today than I usually am, it's because she is so high up that I need wings to reach her."

The little animals looked at each other in confusion. Indeed, they were very surprised. And so they asked, "Who is she? Tell us, tell us, Anathuya!"

"Oh," mourned the likable little skunk, raising his rosy nose, "oh, it's the beautiful moon."

Very sympathetic to Anathuya's plight, the little animals went to plead with Mallcu, the condor, who was the only one of them who might ascend to such heights. They begged the condor to take Anathuya to his love. It was very, very difficult to convince Mallcu to help Anathuya because he kept saying that the little skunk gave off such bad odors. But finally Mallcu could no longer resist the entreaties of his friends and he consented to fly Anathuya to the moon.

When the moon showed her round face in the sky, Anathuya was finally raised on the wings of the Herculean Mallcu until he was able to get so close to his love that he could kiss her greedily with his little pink snout.

Too soon the condor grew impatient and insisted that the little skunk return to earth. There Anathuya suffered much over his lost love. The memory of the sweet kisses of the moon filled him with longing. Happily, since love can be a passing passion, he managed to forget her as the days went by.

But we cannot forget, for the Indians tell us that the smudges we see when we look up in the sky are the marks left by Anathuya's kisses on the face of the moon.

: Thailand

Legend
of a
Child

(Rwanda)

One day a mother wanted to visit her parents. When she got ready to leave, she called her two children to her. She carried the younger child on her back while her little girl of seven walked at her side. The trip was long and they had to travel slowly along an extremely difficult path that cut through a forest of mulberry thickets. The fruit looked so luscious and tempting that the little girl couldn't resist. She plucked some berries and when her hands were full, she ran to eat them behind her mother's back. She continued in this fashion as they made their way through the forest. The mother got used to the game the little girl was playing and didn't trouble herself further. The child ambled here and there, busily plucking and eating the mulberries.

But a strange thing was happening. Each time the little girl had eaten all the mulberries in sight she would raise her eyes from the path and there before her she would see another mulberry bush laden with fruit. Quickly she would swallow all the berries she held in her hands so she could take advantage of the new supply. When she had eaten all the mulberries on the right, another mulberry thicket would appear on the left. The child, fascinated by the profusion of mulberry bushes, completely forgot that she had to catch up with her mother, who never dreamed that her little daughter might stray too far off.

The child penetrated deep into the woods, sometimes going left, sometimes going right, following the pattern set by the mulberry bushes. All of a sudden she caught herself. Shivering with cold, she longed to find her mother but her efforts were useless. The forest was like a labyrinth and it became impossible for her to find the path. Each time she thought she had turned back toward the road she strayed farther from it. Her dainty dress was tattered to ribbons by the brambles and her delicate body was full of scratches. The way seemed longer and longer and longer.

Feeling very spent, she finally collapsed blood-stained and exhausted into the underbrush. Lying on her back, she looked up at the stormy, dark sky. She was so frightened that she broke into sobs of despair.

The mother, meanwhile, walked along innocent of her child's plight. Turning to speak to her little companion, she found her gone. She searched in vain. Frantic with fear, she resolved to turn back toward home, calling the little girl's name over and over again in her desperation. But alas, she reached her house without finding the child. Her husband was astounded to see her return so unexpectedly and to hear her demand without warning, "Where is our little girl?"

"She is not here, but certainly you should know that," said the startled man. The worried mother recounted the events of the day

Morocco

while the father tried to calm his grieving wife. Looking up at the blackening sky, he decided to wait until the next day to continue the search.

During this interval a great storm struck the forest and Thunderbolt, King of the Sky, lifted the little girl up to the heavens. He entrusted the precious child to the care of his ladies-in-waiting. They comforted her with all their hearts and soon she grew well and flourished.

Below them, on earth, the parents of the little girl waited and searched, waited and searched, but they found no trace of their beloved child. They wept pitifully. Believing her to have been devoured by wild beasts, they were, in the end, compelled to resign themselves to the forces of destiny.

Several years passed, and one day Thunderbolt noticed that his little charge had become a lovely young woman. He decided to marry her and she accepted. They started their life together with a magnificent ceremony and wedding feast.

Time passed and all was in perfect order in the sky. Mrs. Thunderbolt had presented her husband with two lovely children. She basked in the sunshine of unheard-of opulence but every so often she would sit on the threshold of her home and sing, "I am lonesome, dear Grumbler of the Heavens. I would like to see mama and papa, dear Grumbler of the Heavens."

Mr. Thunderbolt would answer, "First you must give me another child, dear wife—either a boy or a girl, dear wife—then you may go, dear wife."

Mrs. Thunderbolt waited and when she had presented her husband with four lovely children, two boys and two girls, she repeated her song. Her husband remembered his promise and to prepare her properly for her journey he surrounded her with ladies and gentlemen-in-waiting. He gave her flocks of large and small cattle and presented her with a vast quantity of every sort of food. The servants filled many pitchers of beer. Finally all was in readiness and the procession left the sky on the long, long trip to the home of Mrs. Thunderbolt's parents.

At first the old couple didn't recognize their daughter. They had long since resigned themselves to her death. But when finally they were able to accept the truth, they were delirious with joy. Their daughter gave them the large and small cattle as a gift. She gave them the milk, beer and food and even some of her ladies and gentlemen-in-waiting. And so the parents of the little lost girl became wealthy and affluent, thanks to the daughter whom they believed to be dead: the daughter who became Mrs. Thunderbolt, Queen of the Sky.

Photo: Uganda

The Giant Caterpillar

(Republic of the Ivory Coast)

Long, long ago there was a caterpillar as fat as an elephant. His mouth was as red as his tail. His body was covered with hair and on his head was a long pointed horn.

One day, Mory, Bamba and Badjina went to the field. On the way, they met the caterpillar, who had spread himself across the road to sleep. The children could not pass.

Bamba, who was very well behaved, greeted him politely, saying, "Good day, Papa."

"M'ba,"* answered the caterpillar and moved aside to let him pass.

Next Mory spoke to him. "Good day, Grandfather. How are you?"

"M'ba," replied the caterpillar and little Mory got his turn to pass.

Then Badjina came forward. He wanted to pass too but he was not a well-behaved boy. He was not polite like his friends. He approached the caterpillar and shouted, "Good day, caterpillar." The caterpillar did not answer. He remained as he was, blocking the road with his long, furry body.

Badjina yelled once more, "Red-mouthed caterpillar, I said good day."

The caterpillar did not answer. He did not budge. Badjina screamed, "Red-tailed caterpillar, I said good day."

At last the caterpillar, looking a little redder than usual, got really angry and HOP!!!! he swallowed Badjina in one gulp.

Mory and Bamba were very frightened. They hid in the bush and only when the caterpillar was out of sight did they dare to return to the village.

Badjina's father ran to the chieftain. "My son has been eaten by a fat caterpillar!" he moaned.

The chieftain called all the men together. "Bring your guns," he ordered, "all your arrows, your bows. We must find the caterpillar and when we do, we shall kill him."

The men scurried into the bush. But when they caught sight of the huge caterpillar, when they saw his gigantic red mouth and the long pointed horn on his head, they turned tail, threw away their guns, and rushed headlong to the village without once looking back.

"Why are you running? Where is my son? What's going on?" asked Badjina's mama.

"You couldn't begin to know," answered the chieftain. "That animal is as fat as the 'baobab† de Diamadougou.' His mouth is bigger than a calabash. We are afraid and we are running to save ourselves."

Badjina's mother cried and cried, but the oldest woman of the village comforted her, saying, "Inasmuch as the men can't bring Badjina to you, we women shall go and kill the caterpillar. We shall bring your child home to you."

Quickly the women formed a group. Some carried sticks that pound grain, some brought big wooden cooking spoons, some brought knives that they used to peel yams and others even brought hatchets with which they cut firewood.

As they left the village they made fun of the men. "We women aren't afraid," they said. "We shall bring back the red tail of the caterpillar and the big pointed horn from his head."

After walking for several hours the women found the caterpillar. He was, as always, in the middle of the road. He slept just like a boa constrictor ready to swallow a hind.

Bindou, the most courageous of the women, approached the caterpillar on tiptoe. She took one step, two steps, three steps until she was almost on top of the animal. Then she raised her grain-pounding stick very high, then higher, and even higher and . . . pow! . . . with one tremendous whack she finished him off. "Everybody, everybody come. Come quickly!" she shouted.

The women came running . . . thump! . . . thump! . . . thump! . . . "The caterpillar is dead!" they shrilled with excitement. "Let us open her belly quickly."

And do you know what they found? Little Badjina, alive and unharmed.

The women cut strong vines from the bushes and tied the caterpillar up. Then they dragged the animal back to the village.

"Look, look," they called, "we have found Badjina and he is alive. We women have killed the caterpillar."

"Cut him up in bits," cried all the others.

Alas, with each cut of the knife, ten, a hundred, a thousand little caterpillars issued forth from the body of the fat animal. They crawled on the ground, in the streets, in the village square and even in the houses.

And that is why, even today, we find caterpillars everywhere on the earth.

*Good day, thank you.

†The baobab is a large tree native to tropical Africa. It has an exceedingly thick trunk and bears a gourdlike fruit.

Photo: Rwanda

The Cleverest Son

(Ethiopia)

A long, long time ago an old man who had three sons lived in Gondar. One day the old man fell very, very ill and he called his children to him. He wanted to find out which of them was the cleverest. Speaking softly, he said, "I shall reward the one among you who is the cleverest. There is some money on the table. Each one must take twenty-five cents and buy something to fill my room."

One by one the boys took the money and went out to find something that would fill his father's room.

The eldest son was the first to go. He said to himself, "This is easy. I won't have to look far. There are many things I can buy in the market."

He went to the market and straight away bought some straw.

The second son thought a bit. He wondered what would fill a room. Then he went to the market also and looked through all the shops. It was difficult for him to decide but at last he bought some feathers.

The youngest son thought for the longest time. "What can there be in the market that costs twenty-five cents and fills a room?" he pondered.

For many hours he thought and after much deliberation he went to a small shop on a side street where he purchased a candle and a match.

Next day the three sons gathered around their father's bedside. Each brought with him the gift that he thought would fill the barren room. The oldest son brought his straw; the second son brought his feathers; the youngest son brought his candle and his match.

When the oldest son spread the straw about the floor all were silent. "Only one small corner of my room is filled," said the father in dismay.

The second son showed his father the feathers. They were beautiful to behold but they filled only two corners of the room.

"Is there nothing that will fill my entire room?" asked the disheartened old father.

The youngest son smiled. Quietly he took out the match and lit the candle. Then everyone smiled, for the light from one small candle filled the dark room with a warm golden glow.

The old man was very happy. He looked about him and saw the strong handsome faces of his three sons. But when his eyes fell upon his youngest son his heart was full of rejoicing for he knew him to be the wisest and most generous of them all.

"Though you are the youngest," he said, "you have thought the most deeply and you are the cleverest. I shall give you the reward as I promised. You shall have all my lands and my money. Use them wisely and give your brothers good counsel all the days of your life, my son, for then you all shall flourish."

And so saying, he closed his eyes.

Photo: Israel

the *Giant*

*O*nce upon a time an old couple lived on a small farm. They grew wheat and corn, and owned a few cows and sheep. But in spite of every good fortune, they did not feel happy.

"For whom will all this be in the end?" the husband asked as he sat down to rest before the house when his work in the fields was done.

The wife exclaimed, "If only we could have children so that they could work for us when we grow old."

But time passed and there were no children. Harvest followed harvest and their lives did not change.

One day a woman came begging at the door. The wife welcomed her. She offered her a seat on a bench in the orchard; she gave her a glass of cider to drink and some bread and cheese to eat. When night fell the beggar took leave of the couple, "You have both been generous to me. I shall give you a gift," and so saying, she placed a small white stone in the wife's hand.

"Always carry this on your breast and when you see the moon, show it to the moon."

The wife did as she was told. She placed the stone in a small pouch which she hung around her neck. On clear nights, when the moon traveled across the sky, she brought the stone from its hiding place and let the silvery white rays shine upon it.

One fine day she had a son. The joy of the farmer and his wife was boundless. They made a great feast and all the workers came to share their happiness. There was spirited dancing and the fields resounded with the strains of gay songs strummed on the guitars to celebrate the birth of the little one.

But something extraordinary happened. The first night the child came into the world he cried endlessly.

"Maybe he's hungry," the father said, and ordered a cow to be milked.

The baby drank the pitcher of milk and the onlookers were stupefied at his appetite.

The next day the child rose from his cradle and ran all through the farmhouse. He drank the milk of two cows.

The third day he climbed the trees in the orchard and carried a lamb on his shoulder. His father gave him a leg of beef for supper and he devoured it instantly.

Child

(Peru)

The child's appetite did not decrease. At one month, a whole cow wasn't enough to appease his hunger. Everyone called him Samson because of his unusual strength.

Fear struck the father's heart and he said, "We shall be ruined. Samson will do away with our farm. Let us get rid of him."

But the mother cherished the child in spite of her fears.

"Let us wait a bit," she would say. "Perhaps he will change."

Far from being satisfied, however, the boy grew hungrier every day. In desperation the father would cry, "He'll eat up all the livestock!"

At the end of the first year, the boy was as big as his father. At three he was as tall as a house. His parents could no longer tolerate life with him.

"Go," they said. "Take the wide path that leads to the river. There build a boat and follow the current. After sailing a few days you will find the house of your God-father. Tell him we have sent you to be his helper."

Thus they thought to be free of him, if only for a time.

The boy was delighted at the idea of a trip. His parents gave him

oto: Yugoslavia

their last cow and the giant child threw it on his back as though it were a feather. Samson walked for several days until he came to the edge of the Marañón River. As he set about knocking down a few trees with which to build a vessel, he caught sight of a tiny child making little houses of mud.

"What are you doing here?" asked the child.

"I'm going to build a boat," replied Samson, "but I don't see a tree trunk that will hold me."

"The river isn't very deep," the child said. "You could cross it on foot."

"But I must sail. I have a message from my father," said Samson.

"Before you do, lift me on your shoulders. I've been waiting a long time for someone to take me across," said the child.

"That should be very easy," remarked the giant. "You're quite small and delicate." And he lifted the child to his shoulder with one hand.

Samson got ready to wade the river but the child became so heavy that the legs of the colossus began to sink. Full of fear and trembling, Samson looked up and saw that the little one bore the weight of the world between his extended arms.

The giant advanced a few steps but feeling that he was about to drown, he cried out in terror, "Save me, child! Save me!"

Immediately he ceased to feel the burden. The child became light as a bird and, leaning on the branch he had plucked for support, Samson reached the other side of the river. There the child leaped nimbly from the giant's shoulder and said, "I am the child Jesus. From this day on you shall be known as Christopher because you have carried the Christ," and, taking some water from the river in his hands, he baptized the giant child.

"Now return home, for your parents await you," said the child and disappeared.

Samson-Christopher returned home. His parents, grieving because they had sent their innocent son so far away that he would be lost, rose with joy when they saw him coming and covered him with caresses. They set about finding a whole cow to celebrate his return, but when Christopher had taken the first bite—miracle of miracles— his hunger was satisfied and when his parents set a pitcher of milk before him, only one cup was needed to quench his thirst. The parents looked at each other in amazement. As if guessing their thoughts, their loving son relieved their questioning hearts.

"I have become the same as you because the child Jesus has baptized me. My name shall no longer be Samson, for now I am called Christopher."

And so he remained all the days of his life.

How Women Grew Long Hair

(Kenema District, Sierra Leone)   Photo: Ethiopia

Once upon a time in a certain town there lived a group of women who were very jealous of each other. They all wore their hair short just like men. They were very worried over their ugliness and were always quarreling among themselves. Each time they looked at themselves in the mirror and saw their reflections they became more exasperated.

So one day one of them made up a scheme to harm her mates.* She secretly went and dug a very deep hole in the middle of the road that led to the stream. Early one morning one of her mates took a bucket and set out for the stream. She was going along, singing melodiously, unconscious of the hole in the middle of the road, since it was well covered with dry leaves and a bit of soil. When she reached the spot where the hole was hidden, she was suddenly frightened by a noise from a bush. Startled, she missed a step and fell into the hole. Down she went, shouting and shrieking at the top of her voice.

She shouted and shouted until finally a man came by and started drawing her out of the hole. He held her tightly by the hair and as he drew her out of the depths the hair was growing longer and longer. At last he pulled her out of the hole safe and sound and none the worse for wear. The woman went and told her mates what had happened. The jealous woman who dug the hole confessed to her unkindness and all the mates agreed to grow long hair.

Since then, women grow long hair while men grow short hair.

*The word "mates" in this story means acquaintances.

Challenge of the Sun and the Wind

(Akamba tribe, Kenya)

The Sun and the Wind got into an argument one day. They wanted to see who was stronger than the other. They saw a man coming in the street and they each said to the other, "Well, if you think you are stronger than I am, let's see who is going to make that man take off his coat."

So the Sun told the Wind to go ahead and start. The Wind started blowing and blowing and blowing and blowing and blowing and blowing very hard. The man didn't take off the coat.

So the Sun took over and the Sun burnt his rays down and it was so hot. And the man got soooo hot and he said, "I'm soooo hot, let me go and rest under the tree."

So he went under the tree to rest and before he sat down he took off his coat.

The Sun won.

Photo: Uganda

THE
TEMPERAMENTA

Not only was Tierno a teacher of the children and young people placed in his care, the entire village sought his advice. He was the person whom all the citizens of Bandiagara consulted on all occasions. Sometimes the Master visited the troubled; sometimes they came to visit him. At home and elsewhere men, women and children listened to his words with respect, admiration and gratitude. From the slightest movement, from the least little glance, he could fashion the lesson for the day as it applied to himself as well as to those who were lucky enough to be in his presence at the time he made his observations.

One day a woman of the neighborhood, the worthy Sotoura, came looking for Tierno and said, "I am very temperamental. The slightest things anger me deeply. I would like your blessing, good Tierno. A prayer from you would make me sweet, agreeable and patient."

She had not even finished saying all that she meant to say when her son, a three-year-old toddler who was waiting for her in the courtyard, entered. In his hand he carried a small board. He rushed toward his mother and struck the poor woman a violent blow on the head. Sotoura looked at the baby and smiled. "Oh, what a naughty boy you are to mistreat your mama," she cooed.

"How is it, that you do not rise up against your son, you who swear that you are too often angry, you who deplore the fact that you are temperamental?" asked the wise man.

"My son is only a child," replied the mother. "He doesn't know what he is doing. One ought not be angry with a child of his age."

"My fine Sotoura," said Tierno. "Go. Return to your home. Whenever anyone annoys you, think of the little board with which your son just struck you and say to yourself, 'Despite his age, this person behaves like my three-year-old child.' Be understanding. You can do it in much the same way as you have done it with your son. You will never again be unreasonably angry. Go and be blessed. Cured from your bad habit, you will live happily forevermore."

WOMAN (Mali)

Photo: Korea

Son of the Turtle

(Chinese, from Hong Kong)

Once upon a time there was a turtle spirit who lived deep, deep at the bottom of a pond in the garden of a great and powerful lord. Often, while he basked in the sun around the pond, the turtle's eyes would fall upon the lord's beautiful daughter as she walked silent and alone among the flowers. He fell in love with her and thought to himself, "Even though I am a turtle, I have magic pow-

Photo: K

ers; so why should I not turn myself into a young man and marry this lovely creature?"

And so he did.

The young man was kind, generous and handsome. Not knowing he was a turtle spirit, everyone was delighted with the marriage: the great lord, the beautiful daughter's mother, and most of all, the daughter herself.

In every way the young man was an ideal husband but he had one very curious habit. Every day at dawn he would disappear, not to return until eventide. The great lord, knowing the ways of the world, thought his son-in-law had important business affairs that called him to the Emperor's palace. The delighted young bride did not think to question her loving husband. Only the bride's mother fretted and wondered at his whereabouts. She nagged at her daughter until at last one day she persuaded the young woman to tie a red string to her husband's arm after he had fallen asleep.

In the morning, before the young woman was up and about, the old mother tapped impatiently on the chamber door.

"Has he gone?" she asked.

"Indeed he has," reluctantly answered the young wife as she glanced through the window from which they both could see a trail of red thread. But instead of its going through the garden and out into the thoroughfare as they expected, they could spy the vermilion dash of color among the water lilies of the pond.

The old mother was much excited. Full of daring, she sent the servants to awaken her husband, something she had never dreamed of doing before, while the young bride trembled with fear for the outcome of this strange turn of events.

When the great lord came to the garden he listened to his wife's tale and, turning to his child with a sad heart, he said, "This can only mean that my beloved son-in-law is none other than a turtle spirit. I remember well the day my father placed a turtle in these waters to amuse me, and now we are all led to grief."

The troubled father ordered his servants to empty the pond as quickly as possible; and when the job was done, there was the turtle, lying in the oozing mud, with the red string tied tightly around one flipper.

Feeling a mixture of anger and sorrow, the great lord ordered his daughter to avert her eyes while the men cut off the turtle's head and threw away the body. Then, full of misery, the great lord returned to his house for he knew there was nothing he could do to console his child.

The young wife, suddenly left alone without the husband she loved so deeply, might well have grieved herself to death had it not been for her bright little son, all that was left of her happy marriage to the turtle spirit. In spite of her extreme sadness, she was able to find some joy and a reason to go on living in the good looks and sweet intelligence of the lad.

When her sorrow lifted a bit, she thought to stroll once more in the garden where she had found her love. As she meandered idly through the paths, she came upon the bones of her beloved lying about just as they had been tossed aside so carelessly by the servants. Tenderly she gathered them together and placed them in a silk bag. "One day," she thought, "I shall be able to find a suitable burial place for the bones of my child's father," and, returning to her room, she placed them lovingly at the head of her bed.

A year passed. The old lord died and soon after the old mother joined him in the other world. There was little money, and the young woman was forced to weave cloth which she sold in order that she and her son could share a few crusts of bread. The boy was headstrong and adventuresome. Instead of reading and studying he liked to run about the streets freely with other boys of his age. The mother was exceedingly worried and anxious for her boy's future and often she would interrupt her work to think about what might be done to prepare her little son for life.

In the midst of her meditation she would remember her dead turtle spirit husband and think of his bones that she kept hidden in the silk bag. "Oh that I might find a fine burial place for my dear husband's remains," she would cry softly to herself, for everyone knew that the proper burial place was supremely important to the welfare of a soul that had departed to the other world. The mother wanted very much to provide a handsome future for her son and grandsons-to-be and with each passing day she worried more about how she would manage to find a suitable spot.

One day a seller of burial places found an ideal site. Just above the city, in the middle of the river that flowed through the territory, the currents had formed a deposit of mud. Slowly the deposit took on the shape of a dragon with a head and two very pronounced horns. As time went by, even a long tail formed and in the tradition of dragons, the head began to face upstream. The entire formation could not have been more auspicious.

The grave seller went immediately to the richest man in the city and urged him to purchase this advantageous and unique place. The rich man was wise enough to see the value of this almost magic resting place. He had no doubt that the sons and grandsons of anyone buried on dragon-shaped ground would flourish. He had saved the bones of his grandfather carefully and he had been waiting for just such an opportunity to present itself. The rich man was anxious to take advantage of the extraordinary offer made by the grave seller, but he could find no one brave or strong enough to swim across the swirling currents of the river to deposit the casket in which his grandfather's bones were secured. The grave seller and the rich man were both much perplexed but the more they thought, the more they were confounded. The grave seller feared to lose his large fee and the rich man feared to lose the distinction of procuring this most propitious burial plot. In vain they talked and wondered. Finally, unwilling to give up a chance to do such good business, the grave seller pleaded with the rich man to post a notice offering a reward to anyone who would swim through the torrential waters and implant the bones of the venerable grandfather on the dragon's island. The rich man saw that in this way he might get his heart's desire and although he was not too hopeful, he agreed to have an announcement drawn up offering one thousand pieces of gold and one thousand pieces of silver to anyone courageous enough to carry the casket with his grandfather's bones to the dragon mudbank. A watchman stood beside the notice to bring its contents to the attention of all who passed.

When the people of the town read the notice there was much mockery and joking. "Of what use is gold and silver to a drowned man?" they jeered.

The curious little son of the turtle spirit heard their raucous laughter and came to see what was happening.

"What does the notice say?" he asked the candy man.

"Of what interest is that to you, young fellow?" replied the seller of sweetmeats, and turned away. The little boy followed him and was so insistent that the candy man finally read the notice aloud just to be free of the boy's pestering.

"Oh, how I should like to gain the thousand pieces of gold and silver," said the little boy, much to the amusement of all those who stood about. While they scoffed and made sport of him, the boy reached up and tore the notice down. The watchman came after him to give him a drubbing for his naughtiness, but the boy stepped out of the old man's reach, yelling back as he ran, "I can swim the river. I can swim the river."

The watchman, huffing and puffing behind him, grumbled, "Why, you're only a boy of eight. You could never brave those currents."

"If I didn't think I could do it, would I tear down the notice?" responded the devilish boy. The watchman, much embarrassed by the gawking bystanders, thought he had better take the boy to his master before he himself became the butt of their cruel humor. The rich man questioned the boy in detail, but to every question the boy replied he would be able to carry the casket through the fierce running waters to the dragon burial ground. Finally the rich man and the grave seller were satisfied and agreed to let him try. They set about making final arrangements but in the midst of their rapid chatter, the boy interrupted, "First I must go tell my mother," he said and off he ran.

The two men looked after him with disappointment for they did not expect to see the boy again.

The boy hurried to his mother with the good news. At first she was frightened for his safety and thought to refuse him permission but in the end, remembering that he was the true son of a turtle spirit, she gave her consent. Thinking of her beloved husband, she ran to get the silk bag that held his bones. She placed the small packet in her son's hands and said, "Take this, my son. It contains the remains of your dear father. When you reach the dragon burial ground, place the bag directly in the dragon's mouth."

Promising to do his mother's bidding, the son of the turtle spirit sped back to the house of the rich man, who greeted him with surprise and pleasure. The grave seller and the rich man both led the boy to the banks of the river. They placed the casket containing the bones of the rich man's grandfather on his back and with silk bag that held the bones of his own father tied around his neck, the boy plunged into the torrent.

Like a turtle he dove down, down, down into the deepest water and swam straight away toward the mudbank. He could make out the form of the dragon and, with the eddying of the waters, he could see that its mouth seemed to open and close. Pausing for just the right moment, he popped the silk bag with his father's bones into the dragon's jaws and watched in awe as the throat appeared to swallow and the bones seemed to go down into the belly of the beast. Next he hung the casket containing the bones of the rich man's grandfather around the dragon's horns and, diving into the depths once more, he easily regained the shore. There the delighted rich man awaited him and promptly counted out the reward. Two of his servants were assigned to help the lad carry the bags of gold and silver to the poor mother, who sat weaving and weeping for she feared she might never see her little son again.

Great was her joy when her eyes fell upon him standing once more strong and sturdy in the doorway of her modest home, and even greater was her astonishment at receiving the lavish prize.

True to the ancient tradition that the sons and grandsons of those whose bones are well buried prosper mightily, the turtle spirit's son grew tall and handsome. He was wiser than all other men and when finally he became emperor, he ruled long and kindly over those who had mocked him and called him foolish in his youth.

Once upon a time there was a king in a far, far off country whose name nobody knew. He had only one daughter. She was so glum and sullen that nobody had ever seen her laugh. Although she was quite grown up and pretty, she was so sorrowful and unhappy that everyone gave up trying to please her and left her alone. All day long she cried and sulked.

A Sledge Ride

(Denmark)

In every way the king was an extremely pleasant and clever man, but the problem of his daughter's temperament went straight to his heart. Little by little he became cross and discontented. Here he was with only one child to inherit his kingdom and there she sat moaning and weeping to such an extent that he feared she would die.

Finally the king was so desperate that he issued a royal command that whosoever could make his daughter laugh should have her as a wife and succeed him as king of the realm.

Many there were who came to try their luck, but not one of them could even lure a smile from the princess. Anyone who attempted to win her hand only made a fool of himself two times over: firstly when he came to try his luck, and secondly when he was forced to leave the court in disappointment and disgrace.

Photo: Nepal

Little by little the king grew fed up with all this entertainment, with all the foolish tricks he had to watch, and with all the stupid jokes he had to listen to. Most of all, he was provoked to the point of distraction every time he glanced at the princess with her sour expression.

And so he issued a new command that whosoever tried to make the princess smile without succeeding should be tarred and feathered and turned out to become a laughing stock of the community. This edict made the palace a pleasanter place in which to live, since fewer young men came to try their luck, but it didn't help at all to change the sour look on the princess's face.

Now out in the country there was a man who had three sons: one called Per, one called Poul and a third called Jesper Pert. Their homestead was in a very out-of-the-way place; so it took some time before they heard that a young man easily could make his fortune if only he were very amusing.

Per thought that he was quite comic and as soon as the news reached his ears he wanted to try to win the princess. His mother gave him a full haversack and his father gave him a well-filled purse, and he started off on his conquest in good spirits. Along the way he met an old woman pulling a small sledge behind her. She asked him for a bite to eat and a dime but Per refused, saying that as he was on a long journey he only had enough for himself.

"It will probably be a very bad journey," said the little old woman, and disappeared.

Per ignored her talk and went on his way until he arrived at the entrance to the king's courtyard. Loudly he announced that he had come to make the princess laugh, and immediately he was taken before the young lady and her father. He applied himself to doing some cunning tricks. He could sing the funniest songs you ever heard and he counted on them for his success. He sang one after another until he had sung every song in his repertory, but no smile crossed the princess's face. So Per was dipped in the tar barrel and rolled in the feathers and turned out of the king's court in disgrace. When he got home his mother had to use a whole quarter of a pound of butter to clean him off. She begged her sons to seek their fortunes elsewhere, but Poul insisted that what went wrong for Per might go right for himself and he wanted more than ever to try his luck and seek his fortune. He too received a full haversack of food from his mother and a well-filled purse from his father. Off he went and before long he too met the old woman with her sledge. She asked him for a bite to eat and a dime but he refused to spare her anything because he was on a long journey and had only enough for himself.

"It will probably be a very bad journey," she said, and disappeared.

Soon Poul arrived at the king's palace and when he was taken before the Princess he tried his special tricks. He knew all the funniest tales that existed and they had made so many people laugh he was sure he would succeed. He told the stories well and he even laughed at them himself, and the king laughed, but the princess only yawned with boredom. So Poul suffered the same fate as Per and came home feeling just as miserable and disappointed.

Jesper Pert, however, was not frightened by the experience of his brothers. He wanted to leave home to seek his fortune without letting another moment go by.

"Oh you silly fool," said both his father and mother, "how do you imagine you will ever succeed when your brothers have failed. They are both so much more clever than you. They know songs as well as stories, but you know nothing except how to make a perfect fool of yourself—fool enough to make us both laugh and cry."

"Thanks," said Jesper. "It's enough that I can make you laugh."

Nothing could stop him. He was determined to leave. So his mother gave him some dry bread and his father gave him a few dimes, and with these bare provisions he went on his way.

After Jesper had walked a long while he sat down by the side of the road to rest and eat a bit of his dry bread. Suddenly the old woman appeared, pulling her little sledge. She asked him for a bite to eat and a dime and Jesper willingly gave her all that he had left of his bread and half of his money.

"Where are you going?" asked the woman.

"I am heading for the king's castle to make the princess laugh," replied Jesper. "Then I shall win her as my wife."

"Have you thought of how you are going to do it?" the old woman asked.

"No," answered Jesper, "but I will think of something."

"I think I had better help you a little," the woman said, "because you have helped me. Here is my sledge. As you can see, there is a little bird carved on the back of it, and when you sit in the sledge and say 'Peep, little bird!' then it will run until you say 'Stop.' It turns left when you wave your left arm and right when you wave your right arm. If anyone should touch the sledge, the little bird will say 'Peep,' and if you then say 'Hold on,' they have to hang on, whoever they are, until you say 'Let go.' In this way I think you will succeed."

Jesper thanked her many times for the splendid vehicle. He sat down on the sledge. "Peep, little bird," he said, and it rushed forward as if it were drawn by a pair of fiery horses. All the people who saw him were completely dumbfounded, but Jesper behaved as if nothing unusual had happened. He let the sledge run straight ahead on the road until evening. Then he stopped at an inn to get some sleep. He took the sledge with him into his room and tied it to the foot of his bed, for he feared that it might otherwise run away from him.

The people at the inn had seen him coming on the sledge, and were astonished to see such a conveyance. The maids were especially curious. Late at night, when she thought that Jesper had fallen asleep, one of the maids got up and tiptoed into his room to look at the peculiar sledge. She crept right up to the sledge and touched it.

"Peep," said the bird.

"Hold on!" said Jesper. And there she was, stuck to the sledge.

After a little while another of the maids came silently into the room, and she too touched the sledge.

"Peep," said the bird.

"Hold on!" said Jesper. And another maid was caught.

There were three maids at the inn and they were all very curious, so at long last the remaining one came tiptoeing in and took hold of the sledge.

"Peep," said the bird.

"Hold on!" said Jesper, and there they were, all three of them, unable to get free.

Early in the morning when nobody was about, Jesper pulled out his sledge, and of course the maids could do nothing but follow along just as they were, fastened tightly to the rear. Jesper pretended not to hear or see them. He sat in the sledge.

"Peep, little bird," he said, and off they went down the road.

The poor girls, who really were not dressed to go out at all, had to follow the sledge. They certainly got plenty of exercise that morning!

When Jesper had ridden for some distance, he came to a church just at the time when the priest and clerk were about to enter. The astonished clergymen crossed themselves quickly when they saw the procession passing by and the priest, who knew the girls (he had confirmed them himself), shouted, "Shame on you, girls, chasing a man like that!"

He rushed up and grabbed the one running in the rear to pull her away.

"Peep," said the bird.

"Hold on!" said Jesper, and the priest was caught. He was forced to run along behind the sledge just like the others.

"Lord have mercy on us, Reverend," cried the clerk. He rushed up and took hold of the priest's gown.

"Peep," said the bird.

"Hold on!" said Jesper, and the clerk joined the line.

The sledge came to a forge where a blacksmith had just finished shoeing a horse. He still held the tongs in his right hand. In his left hand he had some hay with which he was feeding the horse. The blacksmith was a happy-go-lucky fellow and he laughed aloud when he saw Jesper and his entourage. As they were passing him full speed he reached out to catch hold of the clerk's robe with his tongs.

"Peep," said the bird.

"Hold on!" said Jesper, and the blacksmith had to hop along while the hay trailed behind him down the road.

Next they passed some geese that came running out to get at the blacksmith's good hay.

"Peep," said the bird.

"Hold on!" said Jesper, and all the geese had to follow no matter how hard they honked.

Finally, the sledge reached the king's castle. Jesper drove directly into the courtyard with all his followers: the three girls in their nighties, screaming aloud; the priest in his robes, praying and puffing; the crying clerk; the blacksmith, laughing and cursing; and the hissing geese. They all made three rounds about the castle yard.

Everybody in the castle, as well as the king and the princess, came to see the weird procession. The king was chuckling with glee, and when he looked over at the princess, she was laughing so hard that the tears were running down her cheeks. When Jesper looked up at her, her face was beaming.

"Stop," said Jesper, "and let go."

The geese, the blacksmith, the clerk, the priest and the three girls each flew off in a different direction. Jesper bounded up the staircase to the side of the princess.

"Now you are cured," he said, "and now you are mine."

There wasn't much anyone could say, now that the princess was happy.

And that is how Jesper Pert won the hand of the princess and came to rule the kingdom at her side.

Photo: Malta

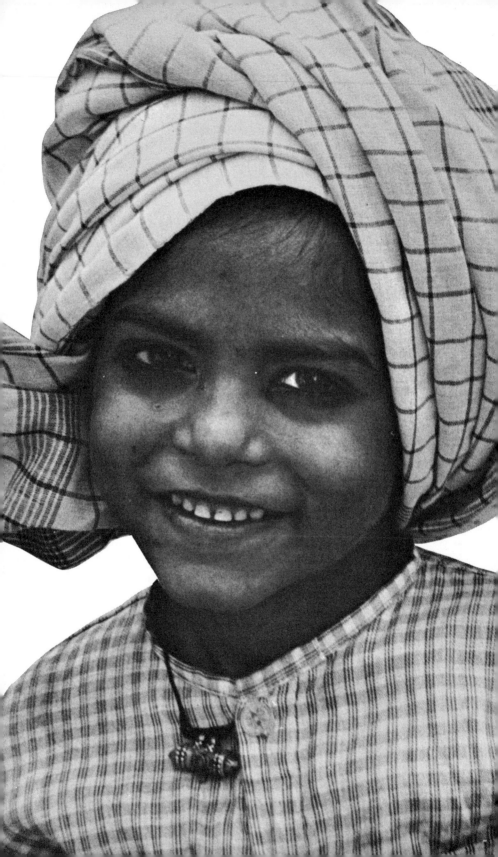

One Sunday morning Gahan's mother decided to go to church earlier than usual.

Gahan begged to be allowed to stay in bed a bit longer and finally his mother agreed. Before leaving her sleepy-head of a son she looked into his room and said, "I'm going to church now, son. Do get up shortly and before you go out, don't forget to pull the door behind you."

"I will, mother," said the agreeable boy and dozed off.

A little later Gahan arose, pulled on his clothes, took a bite to eat, and prepared to go to church. Remembering his mother's last-minute instructions, he opened the door and, with great effort, lifted it from its hinges.

Holding the door by its knocker, he dragged it behind him all the way to the church. People in the street laughed heartily as the boy passed, but he gave no thought to them as he hurried on his way.

When he reached the church he walked in, making such a noise that the entire congregation was disturbed.

His mother, flushed with embarrassment, rushed to his side.

Gahan* Goes to Church

(Malta)

"Whatever have you done, you thoughtless boy!" she exclaimed.

Gahan smiled sweetly at her and replied, "But mother dear, did you not instruct me upon leaving to pull the door behind me?"

*Gahan is the name of a boy who figures in many Maltese legends.

Photo: India

75

The Foolish Hyena

(Senegal)

Fatou: I am going to tell a story.

Chorus: We hear you.

Fatou: Once upon a time . . .

Chorus: It happened . . .

Fatou: That the animals in the bush decided to dig a well.

"I," Kewel the hind said to them, "shall not dig, but I shall drink as much as I wish when the wells have been made."

"Really?" the others said to her. "That we shall see."

Quickly the group set to work. They dug and they dug and they dug. Soon they reached the water table.

Photo: Tunisia

"Now one of us must guard the well," said the animals.

Bouki the hyena, who thought herself to be exceedingly watchful, accepted the job. Everyone was confident she could do it.

"But watch out for yourself," they said. "If you ever fall asleep instead of taking care of your responsibility, you will be thrashed."

So Bouki the hyena climbed to the lookout. However, she didn't take long to fall asleep.

Soon Kewel the hind showed up with her son. She sang, "I am Kewel, Kewel Nduti. I, I, Nduti, do not dig wells but that doesn't stop me from drinking. I, Peulpeul Degnène N'diaye Tioudoum. That goes for my little child too." Then she filled her gourd and that of her child, washed herself and departed.

The next day it was only with the greatest difficulty that the animals could awaken Bouki the hyena. Bouki hastened to say, "What the devil! I slept! Good heavens! That Kewel, no one can stop her from doing as she wishes. Nothing will ever stop her from coming here to drink. I slept a great deal, and she must have come while I slept."

"Get out of here!" the other animals said to her. "You are good for nothing."

The next day Leuk the hare mounted the lookout, after having given his oath to capture the culprit and having received a vote of confidence from his fellows. During the night he too fell asleep and Kewel the hind returned. She sang, "I, Kewel, Kewel Nduti, I do not dig wells, not I, Nduti. But that doesn't stop me from drinking. I, Peulpeul Degnène N'diaye Tioudoum. That goes for my child too." Then she filled her gourd and that of her child, drank and went away.

The next day Leuk the hare admitted his failure and said, "While there is still time, let's find another way to outwit Kewel." He paused.

"What we need," the other animals said, "is to entrust the guarding of the well to someone who can fly down to the very foot of it."

And so Gunoor the June bug consented to take the matter in hand. Gunoor hid himself inside the well. Once again, Kewel came and sang, "I am Kewel, Kewel Nduti. I, I, Nduti, do not dig wells but that doesn't stop me from drinking. I, Peulpeul Degnène N'diaye Tioudoum. That goes for my little child too."

But when she wanted to fill her gourd as was her custom, Gunoor the June bug grabbed her and yelled, "Everyone come! I have captured Kewel."

All the animals hurried to the well. "Ah hah," they shouted. "Now you are caught." Kewel was bound securely but her son was able to escape.

The animals decided to go into the forests to get some dead wood with which to make a fire. They intended to cook their prisoner and have a feast. Once more, Bouki the hyena asked for permission to stand guard.

"I promise you, Kewel the hind shall not get away," said Bouki.

Once more the animals placed their trust in Bouki, but no sooner were they out of sight when the hyena addressed Kewel.

"See here, Kewel, sing me your little song and I will let you go free."

"I shall be delighted," answered the hind, "but only on the condition that each time I sing you will loosen the bounds of one of my feet."

"All right," said Bouki. "Start."

Kewel sang her refrain. "I am Kewel, Kewel Nduti. I, I, Nduti, do not dig wells but that doesn't stop me from drinking. *I, Peulpeul Degnène N'diaye Tioudoum.* That goes for my little child too." Bouki freed one foot.

Kewel sang a second time, "I am Kewel, Kewel Nduti. I, I, Nduti, do not dig wells but that doesn't stop me from drinking. *I, Peulpeul Degnène N'diaye Tioudoum.* That goes for my little child too." Bouki freed a second foot.

Kewel sang a third time. "I am Kewel, Kewel Nduti. I, I, Nduti, do not dig wells but that doesn't stop me from drinking. *I, Peulpeul Degnène N'diaye Tioudoum.* That goes for my little child too." Bouki freed the third foot.

Kewel sang a fourth time and Bouki freed the fourth foot. Then Kewel took three long leaps.

"Hey there," cried Bouki. "Stop or else—"

As she said these words, Kewel jumped once more and disappeared.

With that, Bouki calmly stretched herself out and went to sleep.

"Hello there, Bouki," called the other animals as they returned. But there was no answer. They called a second time. Silence. When they arrived at the well they slapped Bouki a smart blow on her hindquarter. Finally she awoke and said, "Kewel got away from me."

"What did you do that permitted her to escape?" demanded the others in their fury. "We shall eat *you* in her place."

"I couldn't do anything," Bouki cried out. "When you left us alone, you knew perfectly well that she would run away."

The animals replied fiercely, "Well then, tonight we shall dine on you." And that is how it happened that Bouki the hyena was disjointed, cooked and eaten.

And the legend plunged into the sea.
He who tracks it down first will be the first one to reach Paradise.*

*The last two lines of the story constitute the traditional ending of all Senegalese legends.

THE WALLS OF JERICHO*

(Israel)

Photo: Philippines

By Edwin Samuel

Noah is eight; he has yellow hair and freckles all over his nose from the sun. Noah lives on the River Yarkon, north of Tel Aviv, with his father and mother in a white cottage with a red roof. All round the cottage are orange trees belonging to Noah's grandfather in America.

Noah's father looks after the grove. He works all summer watering the trees with water pumped up from the river. Every winter he sends a big box of choice oranges to Noah's grandfather for the New Year. Grandpa is now very old and can't come to Israel anymore.

Noah cannot remember ever having seen his grandpa, but his grandpa remembers Noah as a little boy. Every year now, just before his birthday, Noah gets a wonderful present from his grandpa in America. Last year he got a whole clockwork train. It had an engine and passenger carriages and good wagons and lots of rails and a signal box and even a tunnel. Noah spent hours playing with his new train, together with his three friends: Gad, Uri and Dov. But they had lots of arguments over whose turn it was to wind up the engine. Gad said, "I'm older than you three so *I* should wind it up!" Noah said, "But it's *my* train and *I* should wind it up." Uri, however, didn't wind up the engine very often because he was only Gad's younger brother. Dov, who was the cleverest of all, and wore spectacles, hardly ever got a chance to wind up the engine. He was small and thin, and couldn't fight any of the others.

The four boys are all at school together. Gad is nine; Uri, Gad's brother, is eight; so are Dov and Noah. Noah, Uri and Dov are all in the same class, but Gad is in the class above. He comes to play with Noah, Dov and Uri only because he is Uri's brother.

The four boys are the naughtiest boys in the whole school. Whenever there's a lot of noise or some other trouble, Hannah, the head teacher, says, "I'm sure it must be those *banditim*—those bandits—again."

Like all the other boys in the school, the *banditim* wear white shirts, khaki shorts and sandals. But you can tell at once which are Gad and Uri because they've got red hair like their father, Itzhik, the taxi driver. Sometimes the other children in the school call Gad and Uri *gingi*—redhead—and then there's a big fight. They don't like being called *gingi*.

You can also tell which is Dov because, apart from his spectacles, he has a big cut across his knee. He got it when he fell, trying to

---

*All legends of the Jewish people can be found in the writings of the Old Testament and in the interpretations of those writings that have come down through the centuries. Israel, young as it is, has yet to establish a "new" legendary tradition, and this work by Lord Edwin Samuel is a step in the direction of incorporating the ancient legend into the fabric of the modern Israeli child's imagination.

climb over a gate. It's better now, and he doesn't have to wear a bandage anymore. Dov was very proud of his bandage, and I think he was very sorry when he had to take it off.

One day Noah's father brings him back a big parcel. "Look what I've got for you, Noah. It's from America!"

His mother says, "Perhaps it is from Grandpa. Next month is your birthday."

Noah is very excited. "What can it be? Perhaps it's a bicycle?"

"It isn't big enough to be a bicycle," says Noah's father.

"Could it be an air gun?" asks Noah. "I've always wanted an air gun, haven't I, mother?"

"I don't think it is long enough, Noah, to be an air gun," says his mother.

"Then at least," says Noah, "a frogman's outfit, with flippers for my feet and a mask for my face, and an air-pipe to breathe through. Or perhaps it's a model airplane. I *do* hope it's a model airplane."

"I think it's too heavy to be a model airplane," says his mother. "However, I'm sure it's something you'll like. Grandpa always sends you *such* nice presents."

"Why not open the parcel?" says Noah's father. "Then you'll see what the present really is."

So Noah unties the string. He takes off the heavy brown paper in which the parcel is wrapped. "Oh look!" he says. "There's a cardboard box inside, with *more* string!" Noah cannot untie the second knot; so he gets the kitchen knife and cuts the string and takes the lid off the cardboard box. Inside the box is something heavy wrapped in lots of tissue paper. He tears off all the tissue paper. There it lies, all shiny and new—a big brass trumpet!

"What a gorgeous trumpet," says Noah's father. "I wish I'd a trumpet like that when I was a boy!"

Noah picks up the trumpet very carefully. He doesn't want to spoil its beautiful new and shiny surface. He blows very softly, pressing the various pistons. They make different notes. Some are high; some are low.

"It's a lovely trumpet," he says, "isn't it?" And then he runs out to show it to the other *banditim.*

Noah runs along the road to the house of Gad and Uri, where Dov also plays. Noah feels how heavy the trumpet is. It has a thick red cord attached to it. He puts the cord over his head and across one shoulder. In this way his new trumpet won't fall and get dented.

When he gets to Gad's and Uri's house Noah suddenly gives a big blast on his trumpet that almost blows the roof off. The three other boys come rushing out to see who it is.

"It's Noah," says Uri.

"What have you got there?" asks Gad.

"Oh look! He's got a trumpet," shouts Dov.

"Let's have a blow on it!" says Gad.

"Me too!" says Uri.

"Me too!" says Dov.

"I'm the oldest," says Gad.

"I'm Noah's *special* friend," says Uri, "aren't I, Noah?"

Dov, who wears spectacles, and is the smallest of the four, says, "I don't want to blow your silly old trumpet, anyhow."

Gad tries to take the trumpet away from Noah, but Dov and Uri prevent him. Noah gives more big blasts on the trumpet. Gad's and Uri's mother comes out. She covers her ears with her hands.

"Oh, stop it, Noah! Why don't you boys all go up to the old Arab house and play the trumpet there?"

All the *banditim* run off to the old Arab house. They climb up the hill overlooking the River Yarkon. On top of the hill is a stone house surrounded by a high wall. In one side of the wall is a gate. This house belonged to an Arab farmer. He lived here for years with his family, his servants and his laborers. Now he's gone away. The house is being pulled down to make room for a block of flats. The building contractors from Tel Aviv have already put up a notice on the gate. It says: "Danger! No Admission! Work in Progress." There is an Arab watchman at the gate. Inside, Arab workmen are unloading gravel from a big truck.

The *banditim* peep through the gate. They try to go inside as they have always done before. The Arab watchman shouts at them in Italian, "Run away, boys! Can't you see the notice?"

So the four boys go along a little path outside the wall. They come to a big stone and sit on it—all four of them. Then they discuss what they should do next.

"You know what?" says Gad. "Let's pretend these are the walls of Jericho!"

"Why should we pretend they're the walls of Jericho?" asks Dov.

"Then Noah can blow his trumpet. The walls will fall down and we'll all go inside," replies Gad.

"But why *should* the walls fall down when I blow my trumpet?" asks Noah.

"Don't you know the story of Joshua and the walls of Jericho?" asks Gad. "We're learning all about it in school. I expect *you'll* learn about it *next* year."

"What happened to the walls of Jericho?" asks his brother Uri.

"Well, in the old days," Gad explains, "the children of Israel came over the River Jordan to Jericho. But the King of Jericho closed the gates of the city. He wouldn't let the children of Israel in. So God told them to go round and round the walls of the city seven times. So they went round and round seven times. Then God told them to blow their trumpets. So they blew their trumpets. Then God told them to shout. So all the children of Israel shouted."

Uri, Gad's younger brother, completes the sentence, "And the walls came tumbling down. I heard you learning that bit by heart for your homework."

"You shut up!" shouts Gad. "*I'm* telling the story, not you!"

"So what *really* happened?" asks Dov tactfully.

Gad says, "The walls fell down."

"And what happened next?" asks Dov.

"All the children of Israel went into the city," replies Gad.

"Good," says Noah, "let's try it. We'll walk round the wall seven times. Then *I'll* blow my trumpet, and we'll all shout."

"And then?" asks Uri.

"Then we'll see what'll happen," replies Noah.

"*Nothing* will happen," adds Dov, confidently.

"Well let's try, anyhow," answers Noah.

So they begin to walk along outside the wall around the old Arab house. Gad finds a piece of white cloth. He ties it to a stick, which becomes their flag. As he has the flag, and is the oldest, he walks in front. Then comes Noah, as he has the trumpet. After him walks Uri, as Gad's brother. The last is Dov because he is the smallest, even though he's the cleverest. All four are wearing khaki shorts and sandals. They aren't much protection against the thorns and the brambles through which they must push their way. You can tell from behind which is Dov, as his shorts are covered with patches while the others' are not. But Dov doesn't care even if his shorts *are* patched. He's used to them, and besides, he can't see behind him anyway.

The four *banditim* walk once around the outside of the wall. When they pass the gate, the Arab watchman again shouts at them to go away. When they've got safely round the next corner, Dov whispers, "He's the King of Jericho!" All the *banditim* burst out laughing.

The second time around they *run* past the entrance without being seen. When they're out of sight again, they make long noses at the watchman. "Shall I blow one big blast on my trumpet now?" asks Noah, "and frighten that silly old King of Jericho?"

"No," replies Gad, "you must wait till we've been around seven times; otherwise it won't work."

"After the third time round Dov says, "I'm tired."

"Oh, come on, Dov!" Uri urges him, "you're not so tired as all *that*."

"But the prickles get into my sandals and hurt my feet," Dov replies.

"It doesn't matter," says Gad. "But you just sit on that stone, Dov, and wait till we come round again."

So Gad, Noah and Uri go round a fourth time, and a fifth time, and a sixth time. Then Uri says, "I'm tired, too. *You've* got the flag, Gad. *Noah's* got the trumpet. I've got nothing. I don't want to play anymore."

"All right, Uri," says Gad. "You just sit with Dov and wait for us. We've only got to go round once more. As soon as we get back here, Noah will blow on his trumpet. Then we'll all shout."

"And the wall will *really* fall down?" asks Uri.

"You wait and see," replies Gad.

So Gad and Noah go on marching—Gad with the flag and Noah with his trumpet, while Uri and Dov sit on the stone and wait for them. It's a warm afternoon with no breeze. A thin line of black ants crawls across the path.

While Uri and Dov are waiting, they hear one of the Arab workmen inside the courtyard shout something in Arabic. It sounds like *"Barood! Barood!"* "What does that mean?" asks Uri. "I don't know," says Dov. "Perhaps it's time for them to stop work."

Gad and Noah come round again. They've done all the seven times at last! Their legs are all cut by the thorns, while bits of bramble are stuck to their shirts and shorts.

"We've done it, we've done it!" says Noah. "We've been around seven times! Now, hear me blow my trumpet!"

Noah takes his trumpet and gives the biggest blast you ever heard in all your life. It echoes round the wall. Then all four of them shout together in their boyish voices, "Ho!" A lizard that is watching them from the top of the wall is frightened and dashes away. A moment later there is a tremendous roar and a whole section of the wall falls down! Luckily, the boys don't get hurt. When they recover from the bang, there are still lots of stones rolling down the hillside. A great big cloud of dust rises in the air.

The four *banditim* are terribly frightened. They've knocked over the wall with Noah's trumpet and their big shout. They run like rabbits all the way down the hill. Gad throws away his flag and runs faster than any of the others. Then comes the other redhead, Uri. After him follows Dov, with his spectacles and patched shorts. Lastly comes Noah. He clasps to his chest his precious new trumpet that has done so much damage. He runs slowly, careful not to fall and damage it.

"Wait for me!" he shouts to the others. "Wait for me!"

But the others won't stop. They run and run until they arrive, all out of breath, at Gad's and Uri's house. There they see Gad's and Uri's father, Itzhik, in his taxi. He's just come home. When they get near, he asks them, "Why are you running like rabbits? What mischief have you *banditim* been up to *this* time?"

No one says anything.

"Out with it, Gad!" says his father.

"We were only playing up on the hill near the old Arab house," Gad replies.

"And?" asks his father.

"A bit of the wall fell down," Gad continues.

"And what did *you* do to make the wall fall down?" asks his father.

"Nothing," Gad replies. "We were just marching round it."

"Why were you doing that?" asks Gad's father.

"We were the children of Israel," replies Gad.

"Oh, I see," says his father. "And then what happened?"

Gad nudges Noah, who continues the story. "I gave a big blow on my new trumpet that my grandpa sent me from America."

"And then we all shouted "Ho!" Uri chimes in.

Dov then adds, "We didn't even touch the wall. It fell down all by itself."

Itzhik asks, "Didn't you hear anything *before* the wall fell down?"

Dov replies, "There was an Arab shouting inside the courtyard. It sounded like *Barood! Barood!*"

Uri continues, "Dov said the Arab was telling the other men it was time to stop work and go home."

Itzhik, the red-headed taxi driver, begins to laugh in his big deep voice, "Ho ho ho! Ho ho ho! That's rich! You boys didn't even *touch* the wall? It fell down all by itself, did it? Noah blew on his trumpet and you all shouted 'Ho,' did you? You big sillies, you! Don't you know that when an Arab is going to blow up something—a rock or a wall—he shouts *Barood!* He does that to keep the people away. *Barood* means gunpowder in Arabic. That's what they put under the rock or the wall when they want to blow it up. You're lucky you weren't all killed, you and your walls of Jericho! I wonder what mischief you *banditim* will be getting into next. Ho ho ho! Ho ho ho!"

Photo: Tunisia

Quinde, Bird of the Fire

(Ecuador)

In the time of long ago, before the years could be counted, the aborigines of eastern Ecuador had no fire. Poor things! Squash, beans and yucca were served raw, as were the fish they caught in the rivers and the birds they hunted and captured by shooting arrows through the tube of a long pole. Nor did they have light to brighten their nights or give comfort to their homes. No sooner had the light of day dimmed than men lay on their beds to rest until dawn. They rose early to go to their truck farms and to pursue the difficult task of finding food by hunting and fishing. They knew only that their women and children had to eat.

One man alone, Taquea by name, had the secret of fire. It is not known how the secret came to him, but his wife served his food well cooked and at night husband, wife and children lit their surroundings with torches fed by fuel they made from animal grease or the sap of the wild trees.

Photo: Mexico

One day Taquea's wife went to her garden to pick vegetables for the noonday meal. On her way home she spied a wounded hummingbird lying immobile in the path. The forlorn little thing was wet and unable to fly, much less hover to drive his sharp, pointed beak into the sugary calyx of the flowers from which he drew nourishment. Taquea's wife took pity on the small helpless creature. Tenderly she placed him in her basket and carried him to her house. She set him before the fire so that his powerless wings could dry and grow strong once again. What joy for the little bird! He rolled in the hot ashes and fluttered his fine wings as if he were taking a bath in the waters of health. He felt life returning to his limbs. It seemed that his strength was returning from some mysterious far-off journey. His instincts were as sharp and quick as before and his beak obeyed his head so that once more it became like a needle, straight and true enough to pierce even the heart of the sky.

Some days later Taquea's wife was busy with her chores. She did not notice when the hummingbird stood up on his blackish little feet and shook his wings to free them of the ashes that clung to his feathers. Then, without intent (or perhaps with distinct intent; we know not) he lit his tail with a spark from the fire as if it were a match and flew through the doorway and out into the depths of the forest. He flew and he flew. Far away he perched on the dry trunk of a tree and there he left the fire for those who had none.

Seeing the columns of smoke rising like a thick cloud over the tops of the trees, the aborigines ran from their farms and their huts to the place from which they saw the flames shooting into the sky. There was fire, plenty of fire for all. Had the blessed God Ray remembered their prayers, lighting the immense log in the jungle? Had Taquea taken mercy on them? Seeking the truth, they examined the place. At the edge of the circle of fire, hidden under the vines, they discovered the remains of the tail feather from the beneficent Quinde. But the hummingbird himself was nowhere to be found.

Each person carried his precious share of fire to his hut. There the golden sparks were given new life. Nourished with dry wood, they provided fuel for the hearths. The women immediately set about cooking squash, yucca and beans. They roasted the meat of fish, birds and wild animals. Great was their happiness! At night families gathered round the warm glow of the flames and told stories about the gods, beginning with the story of how the Quinde had written with fire from his green tail—that long tail which from that day to this holds a remaining spark of fire on its tip that gleams like a diamond in the sunlight when the hummingbird flits from flower to flower in his search for the elixir of life.

Photo: Ka

Nasreddin

Hodja

(Turkey)

Nasreddin Hodja lived about seven hundred years ago. He was a highly venerated old gentleman and even today he is respected for his kindness of heart by all those who read about his life. There are numerous tales known as "Nasreddin Hodja's Stories" which point out this famous little Turkish poet-philosopher's modesty, knowledge and wit. Here is one of them.

Once Nasreddin Hodja had a dishonest neighbor to whom he wished to teach a lesson. On a certain occasion he borrowed a saucepan from his neighbor. A few days later he returned the saucepan with a smaller pot inside, explaining that the one he had borrowed had given birth to the littler one. The neighbor, of course, was very pleased and accepted the two pans without comment.

A short while elapsed and Nasreddin Hodja asked for permission to borrow the same saucepan. He took it home promptly but this time he did not return it.

Time passed and the neighbor finally was so anxious to reclaim his saucepan that he went over to Hodja's house to demand its return. Great was his astonishment when Hodja informed him of the saucepan's death.

"Come on now, Hodja," said the neighbor. "Give it back to me. How can a saucepan die?"

But Hodja was ready with his reply even before the neighbor had finished the sentence.

"Your incredulity pains me," was his response. "What is there surprising in the death of a saucepan that was able to give birth to a pot?"

Photo: Greece

93

THE FIRST FILIPINO

(Philippines)

*T*he old story goes that long, long ago our earth was dark and barren. There was nothing to be heard but the roar of the white sea pounding upon the rocky shores and there was nothing to hear but the wind sighing over the sea and the land.

In those times there was a god who lived alone upon the earth. There was no one to share his life. He wandered solitary over the land, enjoying the natural beauties of the island.

One day he thought, "I shall make a man with whom to share these beauties. Then I shall not be as forsaken as I am now."

He thought and he thought about how the perfect man should be created. Finally he took some soft clay in his hands and molded it into the shape of man. He formed it tenderly and with love, for he was sure he wanted to make something important that would bring happiness to the earth.

When he finished the form, the god placed it in the fire to bake. But he was impatient and eager to see the wondrous person he had wrought and when he could wait no longer, he drew the figure from the fire. How surprised he was! He saw that he had not baked it long enough, for the being he had created was the first white man.

"Oh," said the god, thinking of what he might have done wrong, "I should have been more patient. This is not at all the kind of a man I wanted to make. I shall try once more." And so he did.

The god set to work. He kneaded the clay more carefully. He fashioned the features more lovingly—the eyes, the nose, the mouth, the hands and the feet. When he put the form in the fire he was determined not to be hasty nor too curious to let the man bake properly.

"This time I shall not be in a hurry. I shall leave the man in the fire long enough to bake him just right." And with these words the god sat down to wait. He sat and he sat and he waited and he waited many hours until he decided that this time the man would be just as he dreamed him to be. The god drew the second man out of the fire but when he inspected him carefully, he was dismayed to see that he had baked the man too long. The being he had created was the first black man.

God looked at his first man and then at his second. He sighed, "I shall not give up. I must have the perfect man. I shall keep trying until I bake the right kind of man who will live happily with me and share this beautiful earth."

But when he took the remaining clay in his hands he noticed that there was very little left. He knew this might be his last chance and so he began to fashion the man more tenderly than ever before.

"It doesn't matter if he's not as tall as the other two. I shall not mind so long as the features are fine and the color is just right," he said.

The god finished shaping the man. He placed it in the fire with care and watched over it. He timed the baking so that no accident might happen. He waited and waited again but not too long this time, and at last he drew the third man out of the fire.

The god saw that his work was done. Before him stood a shiny, brown man.

"At last," he cried, "the perfect man," and he sang and danced for joy. No longer would he be alone, for he had created the first perfect brown man, father of the Filipino people.

Photo: San Salvador

Acknowledgment

*I am indebted to so many for their
help and cooperation that it would take
a world almanac to include everyone
by name who has made this vast
project possible. To UNICEF in New
York, Paris, and in each of the
forty-two countries I visited I am
especially grateful. To the
ambassadors, ministers of education,
ministers of culture and information,
consular staffs and members of the
staffs of the permanent missions to
the United Nations, UNESCO staffs,
religious leaders, translators, scholars,
individual researchers, writers, parents
and staffs of various welfare agencies
for children who helped in the
collecting of the written material, I
say, "Bless you and thanks." I dream
that all our efforts will help all our
children to a greater understanding of
each other.*

William I. Kaufman

about

William I. Kaufman

WILLIAM I. KAUFMAN's love of children and belief that they are the hope
of the world have led him to take on
the almost impossible task of compil-
ing material and photographing for
this volume in forty-two countries. His
over eighty books on a variety of sub-
jects are published in English, French,
German, Italian, Swedish, Japanese,
Danish, Spanish and Arabic. Starting
in the theater and continuing in tele-
vision, he has pursued a successful
creative life as a communications exec-
utive and consultant, a theatrical pro-
ducer, a writer-editor, a teacher, a
photographer and a song writer.